Just One Friend

Just One Friend

LYNN HALL

Charles Scribner's Sons · New York

Library of Congress Cataloging in Publication Data
Hall, Lynn.   Just one friend.

   Summary: Just as sixteen-year-old learning-disabled
Doreen is about to be mainstreamed into a regular
school, the loss of her best friend to another girl
drives her to a desperate act.

   [1. Learning disabilities—Fiction.
2. Mainstreaming in education—Fiction.
3. Friendship—Fiction].   I. Title.
PZ7.H1458Ju   1985   [Fic]   85-40294
ISBN 0-684-18471-0

Charles Scribner's Sons
Macmillan Publishing Company
866 Third Avenue, New York, NY 10022
Collier Macmillan Canada, Inc.

Printed in the United States of America

First Edition

   5 7 9 11 13 15 17 19   F/C   20 18 16 14 12 10 8 6 4

For Marilynn
with affection and gratitude

Just One Friend

1 I know you aren't real.

My social workers used to ask me sometimes if I ever had imaginary friends and I told them no, that was silly. You couldn't make up a person. I still know that.

But nobody will listen when I try to tell them why I did what I did. They keep asking me and pretending like they want me to tell them, but they get in a hurry and interrupt me before I can get it all out.

You won't interrupt me, will you? Well, you can't very well, if I just made you up.

I didn't mean to do it to her. I would never do something that terrible. It was just, well, it was partly her fault. It was because of the car.

I was over at Robin's house helping her train her dog, the Friday afternoon just before school started, last August. Robin lived at one end of Nordness and I lived at the other end. There were six houses in Nordness, all in a row on the same side of the road, first Robin's house up by the blacktop road, then Dusenburys', Chalmers', Petersens', Osbornes' and Kjellings'. That was me, Kjellings.

My house was the oldest one, or at least it looked like the oldest. On past my house there were just some falling-in store buildings left over from when Nordness was a regular town.

I was up at Robin's house that afternoon, helping her train her dog. Robin was the one I wanted for my friend, but she had Meredith instead. Robin was so cute. She was littler than me and she had short curly dark hair and brown eyes and braces on her bottom teeth. She hated them. She said they made her talk funny, but she still talked way better than me. Faster. She did everything fast.

But I was stronger than her.

But I would never hurt her.

She was the one that started calling me Dory. Everybody used to call me Doreen all the time. Dory is better. It sounds like what you'd call somebody you liked, doesn't it?

Robin had her own dog, Jeckel, an Australian Blue Heeler. At first I thought that meant he had blue heels. Wasn't that silly? It means he is blue-colored, supposedly—really he's sort of gray-and-white-spotted— and that he herds cattle by nipping them on their heels. Jeckel never herds cattle, though; he just gets trained two months a year and loafs the rest of the time.

I just loved it when she trained Jeckel, because she needed me to help her. When I saw her out in her training place that afternoon, I ran right up there.

"Do you want me to be a post?" I whispered.

She was hiding from Jeckel, squatted down behind the lilac bush, and she nodded her head but waved a signal that meant she couldn't talk. Jeckel was lying out there in the grass, panting and looking toward the lilac bush and wondering if it was about time for him to move yet. He hated the long sit and long down commands, because he wanted to be able to see Robin.

He loved her, too.

I stayed outside the fence till the five minutes was up and Robin came out from her hiding place, walked in a straight line across the pretend show ring, then turned a square corner and walked straight toward Jeckel. He put his head down on the ground to help hold himself down for the hard part. He always used to try to jump up when Robin came toward him, and that was bad. He got spanked for it. He was supposed to lie still till she walked around behind him and stood at his right side, and then they both had to wait till I said, "Exercise finished."

Jeckel hated to get spanked, so he pushed his head way down while Robin walked around him. She looked at me and nodded, and I yelled, "Exercise finished."

Jeckel jumped straight up and bounced off Robin's chest, and she hugged him and hugged him for not moving while he was on the command.

3

I'd been helping her train him for four summers, so I knew all about it. I always hated it when the fair was over and I couldn't help her train him anymore. She took him to the dog show at the fair—that was what all the training was for.

See, when we were little, Robin and I were best friends. We were the only little girls in Nordness then, and it was wonderful because I got to be with her a lot.

But then we got older.

We started in first grade together even though I was two years older than her. See, I'm dumb, so they made me wait till I was eight to start school. And after we started school Robin had other friends than me, and they weren't dumb, so naturally she liked them better. And then Meredith started being her best friend.

I don't want to think about that.

After Robin got done hugging Jeckel I said, "Do you want me to be a post now?" That was what I loved the most.

She said, "Sure, we could use more work on our heeling. Wait till we've finished our pattern."

I nodded. I loved watching her and Jeckel do their heeling patterns. They lined up at the starting place, with Jeckel sitting nice and square beside her left foot, twisting his neck around so he could look up at her. Besides his black and gray speckled body he had white chest and feet, and ears that stuck out like handles. His hair was longer than our coonhounds' but shorter than a collie dog, and he was kind of fat, like me. Not round fat, just sort of square-built. He looked kind of like a police dog with shorter legs.

I knew my part. I yelled, "Forward."

They marched forward, right together, just beautiful. I forgot to yell left turn and they had to do it themselves or else run into the fence, but after that I remembered and yelled right or left turns or halts or about-turns. I gave them lots of about-turns because I loved to watch how snappy Robin would twist her body around and reverse her feet so she was going right back on her same footprints, and Jeckel would zip around fast so he didn't get left behind.

I yelled, "Halt, exercise finished," and went over by the flagpole and stood eight feet away from it, facing toward it. Robin got in between me and the pole and nodded to me. I said, "Ready? Forward."

They started walking around me and the flagpole in figure eights. It was my most favorite thing, because when I was a post for her to do figure eights around, she had to walk real close. Sometimes we bumped shoulders as she went around. That made me feel so good.

When we were little I used to pick her up and carry her sometimes, and she used to ride on my back like I was a horse. I smile whenever I remember that. But her mother made us stop. She said my back might get hurt. It would have been nice of her to worry about my back, except I knew that wasn't the real reason. It was because I'm dumb. Maybe she was afraid if Robin got too close to me she'd catch it.

I used to make up plays in my mind that Robin was dumb like me and we could be best friends forever. I tried to make myself be proud of how smart she was in school, but it was lonesome sometimes, always being proud of her and nobody ever being proud of me.

Four years ago when Robin first started taking Jeckel to dog training classes in Decorah, I wanted to go, too. Eldean said I could take one of his coonhounds to the class, and Robin's folks let me ride in with them for class nights. Eldean is my big brother. He's got five coonhounds: Hunter, Bingo, Double Circle, Three Spot, and Elvis. He let me take Bingo because she was having pups that summer and he wasn't going to hunt with her.

The teacher of the dog class was really nice about me and Bingo, but she told me right off, that first night of practice at the fairgrounds, that coonhounds make lousy obedience training dogs. She explained how they have so much instinct about hunting coons that there isn't room in their heads to learn much of anything else. She said every kind of dog is good at something special, like dachshunds can hunt badger the best because of their long skinny bodies, and some dogs hunt lions or leopards or rats on ships better than other kinds of dogs.

She was trying not to say that Bingo was dumb, so I could tell it was me she was thinking about. She knew I was dumb and she didn't want to hurt my feelings. I get so tired of that sometimes.

But she was right. I tried and tried to teach Bingo to walk beside me when I said, "Heel," and to sit down

6

when I stopped walking. I jerked her collar like I was supposed to and shoved down on her butt as hard as I could. After three weeks Bingo couldn't do anything, and most of the other dogs in the class were already heeling and sitting and lying down. So I gave Bingo back to Eldean and just spent my time helping Robin with Jeckel. It was better to help a smart girl and dog than to show everybody how dumb me and my dog were. Don't you think so?

Sometimes I think about what that dog teacher said, about coonhounds not being good at learning obedience commands because their heads were too full of coon hunting instinct. It's exciting to think about it, because I wonder if the reason I am dumb in school is that my head is too full of something else that other people don't have, only I just don't know what it is yet. After all, a young coonhound pup doesn't know about his instincts till he's big enough to go hunting that first time. Then he just naturally knows all he needs to know about following scent and giving voice and treeing quarry. It's his instinct. Jeckel couldn't do it even if he wins trophies every year at the fair.

But then I laugh out loud. I can see myself galloping along on all fours, barking and baying with the pack and chasing a raccoon up a tree. That's so funny.

Still, I am only sixteen, after all. There might be something in my head that I haven't discovered yet, that's better than other people. Oh, I hope so.

Robin and Jeckel finished up their practice, and I

could see she was about to tell me good-bye and go in the house. I hated that part of it. I used to say anything I could think of, to keep her from going in the house when I saw she wanted to. I never get to go in her house hardly ever, so the only time I can be with her is out in the yard. But one time her and Meredith were talking about me in the train station and Robin said, "I don't mind being nice to her, but it's like giving steak to a neighbor dog. You can't ever get rid of her."

After that I had lots of bad dreams about Robin saying that. And I tried not to stay any longer than she wanted me to.

But that day last August I really wanted to stay. It was too hot out to go home. On hot days my mom was worse than usual, and I tried to stay outside all day if I could. If Mrs. Petersen was hanging out wash I could help her hang it or bring it in sometimes. I was very careful not to let anything drag on the ground, so she liked me to help her. Or other times I went across the road and visited Osbornes' horses. There was a long pasture with a creek running through it, across the road from the Nordness houses, and the horses were nice to talk to. The old spotted pony would sometimes come over to me if I was sitting on the ground, and he'd rest his chin on the top of my head and listen to me talk.

Or other times I went for long walks along the old railroad track bed, where the tracks used to be. They took out the tracks when I was little because the trains went broke, but the track bed was still there, and it was a good place to go walking. It was like a long skinny hill about as high as me and just wide enough for railroad tracks. The ties were still there with cinders in between that kept the trees from growing up too bad. If you were wearing your bare feet and didn't want to step on cinders, you could walk on the ties. They were nice flat dark-brown wood, but it would make your legs tired after a while because the ties weren't the right space apart for walking on.

Eldean said you could walk all the way from Cedar Rapids to Minneapolis on that track bed. Isn't that wonderful? But I would get too tired. One time I walked to Decorah and back. Ten miles. But it wasn't hot weather, and I had my shoes on.

In hot weather I usually just walked across the pasture to the train station and sat in the shade, or else went wading in the creek, before I got too old for that.

You can see there was lots to do around Nordness. The only matter was, everything there was to do made me lonesome, and sometimes I just had to go down to Robin's house even if I knew she wanted to get rid of me.

So that day I was trying my best to think of something to keep her from going in the house because I was having one of my extra lonesome days. Sometimes I feel sorry for myself even though you're not supposed to feel that way, and when I do I just want somebody to be nice to me. Mostly Robin. And that day was one of those times.

I started to say maybe we could walk over in the pasture and visit the horses, but just then a car turned in the driveway and Robin let out a squeal like a stuck hog.

It was a car I never saw before. I knew all the cars that lived around Nordness. This one was a little short one with a chopped-off back end. It was the color of apples in July, bright green. Then I saw who was driving it, and I knew the terrible thing had happened.

It was Meredith.

Meredith was pretty, besides smart. She was a year older than Robin and a year younger than me. She had wavy cream-colored hair that used to be short like Robin's, but that summer she was letting it grow long because she could get more boys with it long. She had a perfect figure, too, like somebody on television. Robin was still pretty flat and skinny, and I was like a bag of potatoes. The potatoes were getting bigger, but there were still too many around the middle.

Meredith had greenish eyes and smooth skin. Did you ever notice how some people are made of better quality parts than other people? I mean, smooth silky skin instead of the thick-looking kind with little pin-holes all over it, and bigger eyes and more eyelashes and shinier hair and long skinny fingers instead of short and square. It always seems like it's the rich ones, too.

That's not really fair. It's almost like they made a deal with God before they got born—give me premium quality parts and I'll pay lots of money to your church. It makes me mad sometimes.

One nice thing about Meredith. Some girls who have that light-colored hair wear yellow clothes with it, and the yellow makes their hair look dead because the clothes are more yellow than the hair is. It's like a bird trying to sing over a car horn. But Meredith wore light creamy-colored clothes or else soft green or blue things that didn't yell louder than what her quiet-colored hair did.

Meredith lived across the mile. There were roads every mile, just about. The blacktop that went east and west past Robin's house was one road, and then a mile north was the road Meredith lived on. The short road that went north past the Nordness houses ended after my house, but if you walked out in the bean field behind the old empty stores you could see where it used to run on north to Decorah. It makes you wonder why they build a road and then later on they build a better one over a ways, and the first road has to get all torn up and made back into a bean field. Why don't they just let them be, after they make them?

So Meredith lived one mile from Nordness if you walked straight north, which you couldn't do when the crops were in. If you drove around on the road it was about three miles. But if you knew the shortcuts like I did, you could get there by walking north on the old track bed starting from the pasture. Meredith used to come that way all the time, going to Robin's house.

But now she had a car.

She jumped out of it and ran to Robin and they hugged each other and screamed and jumped up and down in a circle.

They didn't hug me, of course.

But I went over to the car with them while Meredith said, "It's the one I was hoping for, the Pinto. Aren't the seats pretty? It's got a tape deck and everything. I just love it. I'm so excited I could die. Don't you just love it?"

Robin admired everything that Meredith told her to admire. Then she said, "When did they give it to you?"

"They gave me a birthday card this morning at breakfast and the keys were in it. We went to town this afternoon and picked it up, just now. Mom said I could drive it over here just this once. Isn't it fantastic? We can go cruising, pick up guys . . ."

I said, "You aren't old enough to have a driver's license, Meredith. You have to be sixteen."

She glanced at me but didn't say anything. Meredith got a stiff face when she looked at me or had to say anything to me. It was like she didn't know how to talk to me. Robin wasn't like that, but she was more used to me, I guess.

Robin said, "She has a school permit, Dory. That

means she can drive to and from school without a licensed driver with her, but no place else, till she's sixteen."

"Then you can't go cruising," I explained to Meredith. But she didn't want to hear me. She never did, especially when I was telling her the truth.

She turned away from me and said to Robin, "So now you can take your name off the school bus route. You and I are going in style from now on, buddy."

It was then that I finally realized how terrible it was. See, Meredith had been talking about getting a car all summer. I'd heard them in the train station. But it wasn't till then that it finally got through my dumb head that Robin wasn't going with me on the bus when school started. And that was the most scared I've ever been in my life.

Robin and Meredith got in the car and drove away. Robin waved at me and thanked me for helping with Jeckel like she always did. But she didn't stop to think I might like a ride in the new car, too.

That was okay, though. I didn't really expect them to take me along. And besides, I had to go someplace where I could think about my new scare.

2 I crossed the blacktop from Robin's house and went down the ditch and under the fence to the pasture. The blacktop went over the creek right there, on a little old rattly rusty bridge, and there was an easy place to get under the pasture fence because the fence went straight across but the ground dipped down to the creek. You had to get your feet muddy sometimes, but if you wore your bare feet in the summer it was the best feeling in the world when that black mud pressed up between your toes. If your feet are cool you feel cool all over.

But it was August that day and the creek was so skinny I could step right over it, and the mud was dried-up, gray, and crusty. It hurt my feet because it was all lumped up from the horses' hooves so it was like walking on rocks.

The horses were standing under the trees by the

14

train station. I went to all four of them and said hi and brushed the flies away from the wet places at the corners of their eyes. But I could tell they didn't want to bother with me right then. They were too hot and sleepy, and the face flies made them crabby. They'd be that way with anybody, it wasn't just me. I stayed with them awhile and helped brush away the face flies with a leafy twig, but I really needed to think and the train station was the best place for that.

It was right there by the horses but on the other side of the railroad track bed, so you couldn't see it very well from the town side. It was awful little, about the size of Osbornes' garage, but with a steeper roof that had cute little decorations up under the peaks on both ends. They were like cobwebs made out of carved sticks of wood. There was a sign on one end of the station that you could still read if you got up close. It said, "Nordness, Iowa." That was from when Nordness was a real town. Mostly the wood of the station was silvery-gray like our house, which meant it didn't have any paint left on it.

I could never figure out where paint goes when it disappears like that. Does it fall off on the ground, or turn into air like smoke does, or what? Mr. Osborne said you have to put paint on every four years or it disappears, but I've never seen any lying around on the ground. Wouldn't it look silly if a house dropped its drawers like a person does, and the old paint just lay around its feet?

15

To go in the station you had to step up on a cement platform. I can remember when I was so little I had to go up it on hands and knees, but it wasn't really very high. The main door disappeared a long time ago, so you could just walk in. It was two rooms inside, and in the wall between the two there was a barred window that they used to sell train tickets through. In the first room, the floor was all covered with horse manure so old and dried it was just like sawdust and it didn't have any smell. The horses came in sometimes in the winter, but mostly they stayed out under the trees, even in rainstorms.

There was a door in the partition beside the ticket window, and I went through it into my more favorite part. The back room was full of hay bales. Mr. Osborne knocked out the end wall and put a big barn door in it so he could unload hay through, for the horses to eat all winter. He even fixed up a trough right behind the ticket window so when the horses wanted to eat their hay, they stuck their noses through the bars where people used to buy tickets to ride the trains.

I used to watch the horses sticking their noses up to the window, and I'd think how funny it would be to hear them say, "One-way ticket to Minneapolis, please."

The room was full of new hay bales, waiting for winter. They reminded me of the pictures of pyramids in a book at school, great big blocks going up like stair-steps. Only these blocks weren't stone that slaves had to carry on their backs their whole lives and die doing it, just so some rich king could have a fancier grave than some other rich king.

These blocks were a beautiful gray-green color, mostly green, and they were hard and spiky to feel, and tied with tan baling twine so tight you could hardly get your fingers under the twine.

What I like about a hay bale is that from a distance it looks like just one thing. A hay bale. But if you get down on your knees and really look at it up close you can see that it's all miniature flowers and grass blades, with clover blossoms pressed in there and sometimes twigs or even a baby garter snake. Sometimes a baby snake can live through getting baled, but usually not.

And if you close your eyes and stick your nose in, you can smell sunshine. People laugh at me when I say that, but it's true. You can smell sunshine, just like you can hear corn grow on a quiet night in July. You can. It sounds like a lot of teeny tiny creaking noises.

I climbed up three or four rows and laid down on a flat place where I had a good view out the big door. It was my favorite thinking place, and I knew Robin and Meredith wouldn't be using it since they were out in that car, but pretty soon it got too hot, up high in that building. I went outside again and sat on the bank of the track bed looking toward the horses and the houses.

It took me a long time to get around to starting the thinking, because I hated what I was going to think about. Going to school without Robin. In just four more days.

17

I know what you're thinking. I shouldn't be so scared about a little thing like the first day of school, a big old girl like me, sixteen years old, been going to school since I was eight. All I can say it that the thought of it made me sick to my stomach.

See, I was being mainstreamed that year.

When I started in first grade a long time ago, they found out how dumb I was, and when *I* found out how dumb I was compared to other kids, it made me even dumber. I got through first grade by just gritting my teeth and making myself get on that school bus every morning. My mom told me it was the law that I had to go to school, and if I didn't go a big policeman would come and take me to jail. When I said I wanted to go to jail instead of school, she knocked me halfway across the room. And Eldean kept making fun of me, telling me he loved to go to school, which was a bareface lie.

That first day I went to school was the worst day of my life. The only place I'd ever been away from home was going into town for groceries or Laundromat. If I hadn't had Robin to go with me, I think I would have died, I was so scared. My mom was going to take me but she was sick from drinking that day.

Well, the teacher was nice to me, but she was so busy. And later on that morning I had to go to the bathroom. I had to go so bad I was almost crying, but I didn't know what to do, and I knew we couldn't just get up and go out of the room and I didn't even know where the bathroom was. Finally I started crying and the teacher asked me why and I told her, and all the other kids looked at me funny and then they started to giggle.

The teacher said why didn't I tell her I wanted to go at recess when she asked if we wanted the washroom. I told her I didn't want to wash, I wanted to pee, and then the kids laughed out loud and I started crying so hard I wet my pants.

Well, that was my first day at school. I guess things got better after that, but all that first year every time one of the other kids looked at me I could see them thinking about me wetting my pants, and they'd start laughing at me behind their eyes.

Even Robin. But I don't think she really wanted to laugh at me. You know how it is when you're with other people who are laughing. You start laughing, too, even if you don't understand the joke, or if you don't really want to laugh. You can't help it.

But all that year I couldn't hear what the teacher was saying because my head was so full of embarrassment, and when the rest of them started reading and I couldn't, the embarrassment got so bad it was like my whole mind just turned off.

In second grade I had to go to a remedial reading class three mornings a week to try to learn enough to catch up. But I didn't catch up. It was the same way in third grade, and by that time I was the biggest one in the class and that's awful if you're dumb. I was bigger and older than the rest of them, so I should have been smarter. Not just even with them, I should have been ahead of them.

And I was behind.

The older I got, the more I got behind the rest of them, even though I was taking summer school classes and special remedial classes, and trying three times as hard as the rest of them. If we were supposed to read a chapter in our history book, Robin could just fly through it once and remember most of it. But with me, I had to plow through it one word at a time and sound out the hard ones, and I had to concentrate so hard on making out what the words were that they didn't mean anything. Then I would go back and read it again to try to get some of the meaning once I'd figured out the words. Usually I had to read it one more time before it started making sense. Once I had hold of what it was saying I remembered it real well, but it just took me so long to do all that reading. And if we had to get finished before the bell rang I'd get to worrying about going fast enough and then I never would get to concentrate on the meaning.

I hated it.

It was just so much of a struggle that lots of times I wanted to put my head down on my desk and cry, but I didn't dare because they'd make fun of me again. But my head would just hurt and hurt and *hurt* from trying so hard, and then I'd get mad because the rest of them didn't have to work hardly at all and they got A's and B's and C's. For me, a D was good. Not that my mom paid any attention to my grades, but I used to make up plays in my mind sometimes about getting a B.

In sixth grade they did an evaluation of me and decided I should go to this special school. They didn't come right out and say I was retarded, but it was a school for retarded and handicapped and it made me so mad. I knew I wasn't retarded.

I hated going to a different school from Robin. But the new school was real small and they had a van that came and picked me up instead of a school bus, and that was nice. And the people at that school were extra nice to me. You could tell it was their job to be nice to dumb kids, it wasn't because they especially liked me, personally. But still, it was nice to be in smaller groups, in a small building, with teachers that didn't expect very much of me.

It took a while for me to see that I wasn't the dumbest one in the class anymore. In fact, I was the smartest one. At first I loved that! I even started liking to go to school. They had good food and pretty decorations and the teachers seemed happy with every right thing I did instead of mad at every dumb thing, like before.

But I'll tell you, after I was there a year, I figured out that I didn't belong there. Those other kids in that school were lots worse than me. Some of them were in wheelchairs and couldn't hold their heads up right. Lots of them couldn't go to the bathroom without help from the teacher. I mean, honestly. I wasn't like them.

First it made me mad that they thought I belonged

in that school. Then it scared me that they might be right. I started paying attention to how my mind was working. At first it seemed like I was learning better than at regular school because I didn't have to worry about people expecting me to do better than I could.

But at the new school it seemed like they didn't expect enough out of me. They taught me, and I learned, and my reading did get better, but it seemed like I was slipping backwards just because they didn't expect any better of me than that.

By last year everybody that did evaluations of me finally quit fighting among themselves and all agreed that I should be mainstreamed back into regular school. They told me I'd be going back into eighth grade instead of ninth with Robin, and I'd have help from a special ed teacher at the school, but mostly I'd be in the regular classroom.

You know, they're always saying "special." Special school, special education teachers, Special Olympics. They do it to be nice, I know that, so us dummies won't get our feelings hurt. But it doesn't help. They try to make it sound like there's something good about being dumber than everybody else. Something special. They don't really mean it. It's nice of them to try to make it sound good, but it doesn't fool anybody. At least, not me.

One of the worst things about being dumb in a regular school is that the other kids get the idea that you don't have any feelings. Sometimes it seems like they think I'm deaf, just because my mind works slower than theirs. I can still hear when they giggle to each other and look at me at the same time. They think I can't hear "Dummy Doreen" across a room? They think that doesn't hurt?

So I sat there on that track bed embankment and stared at nothing, and felt that old sick scared feeling coming up in me again like it did when I was a little kid. All summer I knew I was going to have to go to the big school in Decorah starting August twenty-sixth.

I knew I was going to have to push my brain as hard as I could again, after three years of not trying all that hard, and I didn't know if I could do it.

I knew the other kids were going to know I came from the special school.

I knew the other girls were starting to get pretty and have boyfriends, and that would be impossible for me, forever.

I knew Robin would be in different classes.

I knew that, in eighth grade in that school, you have to go to a different room every hour of the day. I had never done that before. It scared me. I knew I could write down where to go each hour, but I was going to have to get used to six teachers instead of one. And I was going to have to remember where my seat was in six different rooms.

I might get lost between classes, especially at

first. Robin told me the building was four floors high. I'd never been higher than two floors, and the only big building I was ever in was the K-Mart.

Robin said there were more than a thousand kids in the school, seventh through twelfth grades.

If there was any way in the world I could have got out of going to school that fall, I would have done it. Eldean told me that after I was sixteen it wasn't the law anymore and I could quit school if I wanted. My mom said she didn't want me quitting school, but I knew she wouldn't do anything to stop me if I decided to. She was too drunk and tired most of the time. She didn't even bother with the little kids any more than she had to. As big as I was, she didn't have to bother with me at all, so she didn't.

So I could have quit school. The only matter was, if I quit it would be like I was throwing away all that trying, all those years of me trying my hardest to understand, and teachers trying their hardest to pound it into my dumb head. If I quit it would be like wasting all that trying. And remember how I said I slipped backwards when I started the special school because nobody expected very much from me? If I quit going to school completely, I was afraid I'd slip so far back I'd be like my mom. I couldn't stand that.

I knew, I knew, I *knew* if I wanted to make myself into more of a person than my mom, I didn't dare quit school till I came out the other end with a diploma.

I was going to be better than my Mom. And I knew

what I wanted to be. A waitress. That was the other reason I couldn't quit school. I knew it was going to be hard to get a waitress job in a good place because of being dumb and kind of fat, but I figured if I had that high school graduation diploma I would prove to the restaurant people that I could learn, and work, and stick with it.

' I'd never been in a restaurant, just the drive-in one with Eldean a couple of times, and they didn't have waitresses. You just drove up to a big board with the menu on it and told the voice in the board what you wanted, and when your car got up to the window your food was all ready for you in a bag.

But I watched *Alice* on television every afternoon at five o'clock, and I knew I wanted to be a waitress. It's so clean in a restaurant. And the waitresses have fun together, like a family. Like friends. They go to each other's apartments after work and if one of them gets in trouble the other ones all help out.

And I was sure I could do the work. You don't have to read very much. You go up to the people as soon as they sit down, and bring them water and place mats and menus. You smile and say nice weather for this time of year, or something like that, and when they decide what they want to eat you write it down. You give the ticket to the cook and he has to do all the main work. All you have to do is carry the plates back to the table and if you are fast and clean and smiley, they give you extra money. I knew I could do all that.

If you're a waitress you make enough money to live someplace all by yourself and buy clothes and magazines and your own television set. That would be the best way in the world to live, and I was dead set on getting it for myself.

So I had to go to that big school August twenty-sixth. I had to.

And now that Meredith had her car, I was going to have to go alone.

I couldn't stand my sick scared thoughts anymore. Besides, the sun was getting down toward the tops of the trees on the ridge behind Nordness, which meant it would be time to watch *Alice* pretty soon. So I told the horses good-bye and started home.

While I plodded across the chewed-off grass of the pasture I started thinking that maybe there would be some way of stopping Robin from riding to school with Meredith, at least that first day, till I found my way around.

I decided to exercise my brain and try to figure out a way.

3 I went around by the back door so I could see what kind of mood the dogs were in. All five of them had their own houses. Bingo and Three Spot and Hunter had oil drums to live in, and Double Circle and Elvis were chained to an old junk car body, one on each side. They slept on the back seat. It got awful cold for them in winter. I told Eldean that but he didn't pay any attention.

I could tell from looking at the dogs that Eldean was taking them hunting that night. How in the world they could read his mind like they did, I'll never know, but every time he took them out, they knew all day ahead of time, and they paced back and forth as far as their chains let them, and whined and whined. They were big tall dogs with long heads and ears and legs and tails, and short hair.

Sometimes our landlord yelled at Eldean about all those holes in the backyard where the dogs dug out cool places in the dirt to lie in. But Eldean told him if it wasn't for the dogs where would we get the rent money, and that was the truth. Eldean went coon hunting maybe two or three nights a week, all night, and he'd get seven or eight coons a trip if he was lucky. The fur buyer's truck came around once a month and the man paid Eldean fifteen or twenty dollars each for the coon pelts, and that was what got us our rent money and bought gas for Eldean's pickup truck.

My mom got her ADC check every month; that was what the state paid her for having babies. But by the time she bought groceries and booze, there wasn't any left for anything else. The neighbors usually gave us our clothes.

I hated living like we did. We were the only poor family in Nordness. All the rest of them had regular jobs—Mr. Osborne taught at the college in Decorah, and Mr. and Mrs. Dusenbury had a bakery, and like that. It just made me more and more sure I wanted a regular job, every time I thought about it.

So now the problem was how to get Robin to go to school with me that first day, so I could stand the scariness of it.

I stood with my hand on Bingo's head, staring at the old junk car that Elvis and Double Circle were chained to. If I had a car of my own . . .

No. I wouldn't know how to drive it. And where would I get the money to fix that old car up? It didn't even have an engine or doors or wheels.

28

And even if I had a good car and knew how to drive it, Robin would still rather go with Meredith. They were friends.

Sometimes I just got so jealous of that. It wasn't that I didn't want other people to have friends, it was that I wanted *me* to have one, like everybody else did.

I went on in the house. My mom was sitting staring out the living room window where she always sat, just like she expected to see traffic going by or people walking past or something. No traffic ever went by. The only people that ever walked past were her own kids. She was a big fat woman, much fatter than me. She hardly ever got out of that brown chair by the window.

The little kids were playing on the floor. I stepped across their play and turned the television set from their cartoons to my program. *Alice.* They didn't care. Two of them weren't watching anyhow and the other two would watch anything that was on.

I sat down on the floor and automatically opened up my arms for Bobby to curl up in my lap. He was four, and he hadn't started talking yet. I thought there was something wrong with him, but my mom didn't seem worried. He liked to be held a lot and I liked having somebody to put my arms around.

We sat there for the whole half hour with Bobby's head on my chest, thumb in his mouth, his heels bopping against my legs. It was a good story. Alice and Flo and Vera and Mel all got locked in the storeroom together without any can opener to open all the cans of food on the shelves, so they were hungry and mad at each other.

The program didn't have very many scenes where Alice was waiting on customers, though, and that was my favorite part because I was trying to learn all about being a waitress from just watching that program.

Eldean drove in from somewhere after the program was over, and he and I fed the little kids some supper, cereal and baloney-on-cracker sandwiches. Mom's ADC worker kept telling her she had to quit feeding us that kind of food because it made us fat and didn't give us any energy, and it made our brains work slower. She told my mom to buy green vegetables and meat and fresh fruit, but Mom said there wasn't enough money to fill us up with that kind of food.

That was another reason for wanting to stay in school till I graduated. The school lunches were the only good food I got, and I could always tell a difference in myself in the summer. I'd get heavier feeling, like I didn't have the strength to carry myself around. You'd think I eat a lot, because of being fat, but I don't. And I have tried not to be fat. I tried doing exercises. I tried for eight days in a row, but I would get so out of breath I couldn't do them, and I was still just as fat. But I did try.

When we got the little kids taken care of, Eldean and I sat down and ate together. Sometimes he could be almost like a friend. He was tall and skinny and had dark hair, kind of good-looking, I thought. He didn't look anything like me. My mom said Eldean and I had different fathers. She never said much about any of us kids' fathers and we didn't ask. I figured they can't be much better than she is, so I didn't want to know. I just had to be my own person, not somebody's daughter.

I said, "Eldean, can I go coon hunting with you tonight?" I don't know why I asked. He never took me and I didn't really want to go. He looked up from his cereal bowl and snorted and went on eating.

I said, "When school starts next week, would you take me?"

"That's what we got school buses for," he said through a mouthful.

"I know it, but I'm scared to go alone. That's a big building. I won't know where to go when I get there. Please, Deanie?"

"Robin'll show you where to go."

I shook my head. "She's not going to ride the bus. Meredith got a car for her birthday and Robin's going to ride to school with her all year. She's taking her name off the school bus list."

"What'd she get?"

"Huh?"

He looked impatient. "What kind of car'd she get?"

"I don't know. A green one with a chopped-off back end."

"A green one? I ask you what kind of car and you tell me a green one? Doreen, you are something else, you know that? Throw that baloney down here once."

31

Sometimes Eldean was like a friend. Not always.

"You could take me to school just the first day, couldn't you? You went to that school, you know your way around inside it." My voice was begging.

"I said I'd never go inside that place again, and I meant it." He looked at me, and we both remembered him getting caught breaking into the school building five years ago when he was fifteen. He and another guy were trying to get at some money that was supposed to be in the office overnight, from selling activity tickets. They sent him to the Boys Training School at Eldora, which was supposed to straighten him out. It was partly a school and partly a jail, I guess, from what Eldean said. He was there three years till he was eighteen and they had to let him loose.

Maybe it did straighten him out in a way. He learned welding there. But he was never able to get many jobs and usually he quit or they fired him after a few weeks if he did find a job, and then he'd be back to coon hunting, which he liked better than welding anyhow.

He made lots of money when Bingo had pups. If he grew the pups out and trained them he could get six hundred dollars for one pup. That was where he got the money to buy his pickup. He figured Mom wouldn't live to much of an old age since she was so fat and drank so much and didn't hardly ever move around, and he knew the little kids would all be grown and gone or else in an institution someplace before long. And I was only a few years away from being on my own some way or another. So he figured on having the whole place to himself, and a nice life coon hunting and selling dogs.

I wished I was that far along on my dreams.

"Just the first day," I begged again.

He said, "Why don't you ride to school with Robin and Meredith, in her green car?"

See what I mean about how dumb I am? I never even thought of that. I was so relieved, and then so excited, about him solving my problem, I ran out and headed up the street toward Robin's house right then and there.

All the way up the street I planned what I would say. I was nervous in my stomach. If Robin was on my side, I knew she would talk Meredith into letting me ride with them, but if she wasn't, that would be the end of that.

Robin's house was a cute little white house with blue shutters and pretty trees and bushes around it. It was on the side of the hill, with a white fence around the yard, which went downhill from the house to the creek. It looked like the kind of house that would be in a picture book.

I went around to the back door and knocked. Robin's mother came to the door. She was nothing like my mom. She was little and skinny like Robin, and pretty. I said could I talk to Robin and she said yes, wait just a minute, she'd call her. I could tell from the sounds behind her that they were eating supper. I shouldn't have come. I should have waited till tomorrow and watched for Robin to come outside. But it was too important. I couldn't wait.

Robin's mom didn't ask me to come in, but she went and got Robin, who came to the door with her fork still in her hand. I knew from that, she'd rather be back eating than talking to me, so I tried to make it fast.

"Hi," I said.

"Hi, what do you want, Dory? I'm eating."

"Um, I was just wondering if maybe I could ride to school with you and Meredith in her car? Do you think?"

Robin looked uncomfortable, like she wanted to get away from me. My whole insides just sank down.

"I couldn't say that," Robin said. "It's not my car. I couldn't invite someone else to ride in it."

"I know, but could you just ask Meredith? Please, would you?"

"Why, though? Wouldn't you rather ride the bus with all the other kids?"

I shook my head, but I couldn't explain. My feelings got all tangled up in my chest and they wouldn't let the air come through. Robin was never afraid of anything in her life. She wouldn't understand if I told her I was scared to death of high school. She wouldn't understand.

I just stood there shaking my head and trying not to let tears come in my eyes. That would really make

her want to get away from me if she thought I was crying about it. Like a big old fat baby.

"I can't promise rides in somebody else's car,"
Robin said again. She was wishing I would leave, but
I couldn't yet.

"Would you ask Meredith?" I begged.

"Ask her yourself."

"I can't."

"Why not?"

Again I just shook my head. How could I tell her
I was afraid of Meredith because of how she looked at
me with her stiff face and tried to pretend I wasn't
there?

I couldn't explain to Robin, but I couldn't leave,
either, so I just stood there being sad till finally Robin
said, "Okay, I'll ask her. But don't count on it, okay?"

I smiled so hard my cheeks almost pushed off my
face.

"Okay."

I turned around and headed for home. But on the
way I stopped to talk to Mrs. Osborne while she washed
her car, and that took a while because it's hard to talk
over the noise of the water. Mostly I just watched while
she squirted it with the hose and rubbed it with a big
sponge.

Since I was still thinking mostly about Robin and
the school problem I looked down toward Robin's house
every now and then, and that's how I happened to see

her run across the road and down the ditch into the pasture. She hopped across the creek and headed straight for the train station, and I knew she was going there to meet Meredith. Robin never went there alone to think, like I did. She didn't have to. Her brain worked so good she could think while she was doing other things and talking to people. I was so jealous of that sometimes.

I waited till she was out of sight over the track bed embankment, then I headed that way myself. Most of what I knew about Robin and Meredith I found out from listening to them when they met at the train station to talk about stuff they didn't want to say over the phone in front of their families. And this was going to be too important to miss out on.

Meredith was coming down the track bed from her house when I got to the horses, so I ducked down among the horses' bodies and watched from under Rebel's belly and got switched in the face by his tail while I was at it. When Meredith jumped down off the embankment and disappeared, I went on over there.

They were in the hay room, as usual. I snuck in by the main door and eased myself down on the dried manure on the floor, with my back to the partition and my ears wide open.

Meredith said, "What's up?" I heard her dropping down on a hay bale.

"Dory problems," Robin said. "I didn't want Mom

to hear. Dory wants to ride to school with us in your car."

"Oh, rats," Meredith sighed.

"She came over tonight while we were eating supper and asked if she could. I told her she'd have to ask you, it's your car."

"Thanks a bunch, buddy."

"She won't ask you. I think she's scared of you or something."

Meredith snorted a little laugh.

Robin said, "I don't know. I feel sorry for her. Lord knows she'd turn herself inside out for me if I asked her to. She's been that way since we were little kids. I've never done a thing nice to her, or for her, our whole lives, and yet she's got this worship thing for me. It's a real . . ."

"Pain in the butt."

"Well, I wasn't going to say that exactly. I mean, I like Dory. She's very sweet in her own weird way, you know? But I mean . . ."

"We don't want her hanging around our necks when we start school," Meredith said flatly.

"Well . . . no, not really. I mean, Lord, it's hard enough to be popular when you don't have anything going against you. I know it isn't fair, but other kids do judge you by the friends you keep." Her voice sounded miserable. "I guess I just don't want people thinking Dory Kjellings is my friend."

That hurt me so bad when she said that.

They didn't say anything for a while. I thought about her saying she liked me, and especially about her saying I was sweet. That made me feel so good. Why did she have to spoil it by saying she didn't want people thinking I was her friend?

But then I realized something. What she said was, she didn't want people to *know* I was her friend. That meant I *was*. That meant she thought I was her friend, didn't it? I started getting this glowy feeling, right then.

Meredith started talking again. "Well, she's not riding in my car. I don't care, she's just not."

"What am I supposed to tell her?" Robin sounded sad.

"How should I know? She's your buddy. Tell her it's a little car and there's not enough room for three people."

"Mare, she saw the car. She knows it's got a back seat. She's not that dense."

"Well? Tell her something. I don't care what. But I didn't get that car to be hauling all the poor white trash in the neighborhood to school and back. I got it so you and me could go where we want, when we want, just us alone or whoever we want with us. That does not include Dory Kjellings."

They started talking about what classes they were going to take, so I crawled to the door and got out of there. I walked slow, across the pasture. It was almost dark by that time, and there was a nice breeze. It was my favorite time of the day usually, but now I was so full of thoughts and feelings I couldn't enjoy it. I jumped the creek, climbed the ditch beside the bridge and sat down on the edge of it with my legs hanging over. I leaned my forehead against the rusty metal braces of the railing and turned my thoughts loose.

One thing. Robin was almost on my side. Meredith was my enemy but not Robin, not really. When I looked at it from Robin's mind I could understand why she wouldn't want people to think I was her friend. People like her don't usually run around with people like me. I knew that.

But yet, she liked me. She said I was sweet.

Sweet.

That made my eyes get wet when I thought about her thinking I was sweet. My heart just swelled up and made my chest ache, I wanted to be friends with her so bad.

I got my mind away from that and started working on how I could get Robin away from Meredith. That seemed like the best thing to try to do. If Meredith wasn't Robin's friend, then maybe there would be room for me in between them, because I knew from what Robin said in the train station just then that she liked me. It was only Meredith that got in the way of Robin being my friend. So, what I had to do was make them not be friends any more. Then there would be room for me in between them.

And Robin wouldn't ride to school in Meredith's car.

By the time Robin started across the pasture toward home it was almost too dark for her to see. She didn't notice me till she was stepping across the creek, almost under the bridge.

"Hi," I said.

She jumped about a mile. "Hi, Dory." She ducked under the fence wire and sort of hurried up, climbing the ditch, like she didn't want to talk to me.

I said, "I changed my mind."

"What?"

She stopped by the side of the road and turned to look at me. She was like the colt, two years ago when he first got born in the pasture and he looked at everybody with his big eyes, trying to understand if we were going to hurt him or not.

"I changed my mind. I don't want to ride in Meredith's car. I want to ride on the bus like I was going to."

Even as dark as it was, I could see her face get softer and happier. It was like I gave her a present. That made me feel so good. See, I knew Robin would hate to tell me a lie. She hated to tell lies. So do I, but I told her that one so she wouldn't have to make up a fib to me about why I couldn't ride in Meredith's car.

"Oh," she said. "Okay." She looked like she wanted to say something more, but couldn't. I sure knew how that felt. When she did say it, it was so wonderful it made me swell up with happy air inside me.

"You want to ride in with us to the fair tomorrow, cheer Jeckel and me on to victory?"

"Yes!" My cheeks almost fell off my face again, I was smiling so hard.

"Okay. We're going to leave at five. Come on down then."

She went on across home, but I sat out there on that bridge for a long long time, swinging my legs and flying inside.

Way off south I heard Eldean's hounds in cry, and I knew some coon had just made a one-way trip up a tree. Usually that bothered me, but tonight I was too happy.

I was about to get a friend.

4 That night I slept on a blanket on the bedroom floor. My little sisters were just too hot in that bed. I was the heaviest one, so they always rolled toward me in the middle as soon as they fell asleep, and they cut off all my air. And besides, I needed to feel like I was alone, so I could do some serious thinking.

The floor was awful hard but there was a little breeze in from the window, and I guess you can't have soft and cool both in this life. I made a pillow roll out of my shorts and tee shirts so my head wouldn't be on the hardness, and spread out all my arms and legs and fingers and toes for the breeze, and got busy with my problem.

How to make Robin and Meredith not be friends anymore.

I thought a long long time about why people are friends with each other in the first place. Two reasons,

I figured. One, you live in the same neighborhood and you're the same age. Well, they did and they were, and there wasn't anything I could do about that. Two, you like somebody because they like you.

There. That was it.

All I had to do was make Robin think Meredith didn't like her, and then make Meredith think Robin didn't like *her*, and first thing you know, they wouldn't be friends anymore.

But here it was going on Saturday, and school started Tuesday. Not very much time to break them apart. And how could I do it, anyway? If I just told each of them that the other one didn't like her, they wouldn't believe me. They'd know better. Then they'd laugh at me all the worse.

I thought on that problem for a long long time, and finally came up with how to do it. Figure out something bad about each one of them that was really true, and pretend the other one said it. That way, they might believe it.

Okay. Do the easy one first. What was bad about Meredith? She was boy crazy and stuck-up. Now, what was bad about Robin?

Nothing.

Okay, pretend I'm Meredith looking at Robin. What would I maybe think was bad about Robin if I was Meredith? If I was Meredith, prettiness would be the most important thing about myself, so that's probably what would be the most important thing about somebody else, too. If I was Meredith I might not think Robin was as pretty as me because she wore braces and didn't have any figure yet.

Or I might thing she was babyish because she still loved to do things like training her dog, instead of chasing boys.

A sweat of relief and excitement came out all over my skin and made me feel chilly in the breeze. It took me a long, long time to fall asleep.

I was glad I slept so late in the morning, because it made less hours to wait till five o'clock. I spent most of the day getting ready. First I dug out my summer dress from the pile of dirty clothes waiting for Mom or Eldean to take them to the Laundromat. The dress had some ripped places under the arms so I took it next door to Mrs. Osborne, and she sewed it for me on her electric sewing machine. I loved to watch that thing whiz along. You wouldn't believe how fast she went on it.

When I told her I was going to the fair with Robin that night to watch Jeckel in the dog show, she said I could throw the dress in with a load of her wash that she was about to do. She didn't usually make offers like that for fear she'd end up doing all our wash, and with four little kids plus us three big people, well, no neighbor is going to let herself in for that. But I guess she saw how excited I was about the fair. She was really a nice lady.

44

I sat out on her back steps for the hour it took to wash and dry the dress, so I wouldn't be on her nerves. I liked looking at her backyard, anyway. It was all neat, with nice flat mowed grass that looked like they cleaned it with a vacuum cleaner, and flowers around the edges. Behind all of our backyards there was a pasture fence and then a steep uphill covered with trees and rocks, so our yard had sunset about the middle of the afternoon.

Eldean was in our backyard, skinning out the coons he got last night and tacking up the pelts on stretcher boards to hang up in the shed to dry. The little skinned corpses he fed to the dogs. He was whistling away like crazy. Eldean was a happy person. I think it was because he was in charge of his own life. He didn't have to do anything he didn't want to.

I'm going to get like that.

Just make it through school and into a waitress job.

When Mrs. Osborne handed me my dress, all folded and clean and warm, she got kind of a hard bright sound in her voice like she was embarrassed, and said, "Now you'll have to take a nice hot bath and shampoo your hair so you'll be all set for this evening."

I got so red all over I couldn't move. I knew everybody thought I was dirty just because I was fat, but I really did try. The only matter was, we didn't have any hot water at our house because it cost too much, and sometimes in the winter I hated to wash my hair because of the cold water and the cold house with all the drafts it gets in wintertime. But in the summer I washed myself all over every night with a washrag, which was more than anybody else in our family ever did. And I washed my hair, too, but Mom never had enough money to buy regular shampoo so I had to use dish soap and it left about as much sticky in my hair as what it got out. I cut my hair myself whenever it needed it, and I thought I did a very good job. My hair had some natural curl in it, so it never looked completely bad.

But even as hard as I tried everybody always thought I was dirty. And I wasn't. It made me so mad, and so embarrassed.

While I was standing there trying to think of something to say, Mrs. Osborne said, "I have some new bubble bath, Dory. Why don't you take your bath here, and try it out. Would you like to?"

I hated the idea of taking my clothes off in a strange house, but it was too good of an offer to pass up. She took me in the bathroom and showed me how to work the faucets and the shower part, and gave me bubble bath and shampoo and hair conditioner. I wondered if that was something to make your head cool, like "air conditioner." That made me laugh inside myself.

My first hot bath of my whole life, not to mention bubble bath. It felt so good I almost cried. The bathroom was all pink, even the tub and sink and john. It was just like in a dream, with all that white fluffy bubble bath all over me like a lace bathrobe. Silk and lace.

I let my arms float on the water and made up a play in my mind. In the play, Robin and I were living together in our own little house. No. No, in a beautiful apartment like Alice. I went away to work all day in my waitress job and Robin went to work all day in her . . . let's see . . . dog trainer job. Then in the evenings we would take long baths in hot water and bubble bath, and fix each other's hair. And cook fancy meals in our cute little kitchen. And watch TV all night on a big color TV set. And we'd have lots of friends, like Flo and Vera and Mel from work, but her and me would be a pair and nobody could ever break us apart.

Like I was going to do to her and Meredith.

I got half excited and half sad, thinking about what I was going to do. Excited hoping it would work, and sad knowing it was going to hurt Robin's feelings for a little while, but then she would have me for her friend so she wouldn't need Meredith anyhow.

I took my underwear in the bathtub with me and scrubbed it in the bubbles. I knew I'd have to wear it wet for a while till it dried off, but that was okay. I wanted to be completely clean all over for going to the fair with Robin and her family. They might think I was dumb and fat and there was nothing I could do about that, but I was damned if they were doing to think I was dirty, too.

I made myself wait till just before five, till I started up the road to their house. They were all getting in the car, her mom and dad in front, Robin and Jeckel and me in behind. It was perfect. They all said hi as I climbed in, and everbody acted excited and happy.

Robin looked so cute. She was wearing her 4-H tee shirt with the green four-leaf clover on the chest, and green slacks and new white tennis shoes and a red plastic band on her wrist that meant she was a 4-H member and didn't have to pay to get in at the fair gate.

I had my money all ready in my canvas shoulder bag, three dollars that Eldean gave me.

We started out the driveway and turned the wrong direction. "That's the wrong direction," I said to Robin's dad.

Robin said, "We're going by to pick up Meredith."

"Oh." I sat back, half disappointed because Meredith was going to be horning in, but half excited because it would give me my chance to say the bad thing to Meredith about Robin.

Meredith's house was a big fancy brick one with a long lane leading up to it. It was just a farmhouse, I always told myself whenever I saw it. Meredith's dad was just a farmer. But still, it made me feel little and cheap, looking up at that big brick house. It was like a mansion in a story. Even the barns were beautiful.

She came out and got in beside Robin, who had to hold Jeckel on her lap to make room. Meredith frowned over at me like she was surprised to see me there beside her friend. And didn't like it very much. I got real cool and smiled back at her frown, and she didn't like that, either.

But did she ever look pretty! She had matching slacks and shirt, sort of soft blue-green like only expensive clothes can be. The cheap ones are always bright colors, if you ever noticed. You have to go someplace better than K-Mart to get soft pretty colors like that.

I added another part to the play in my mind. Besides Robin and a pink bathroom and color TV, clothes with soft colors in them.

All the way to Decorah, Robin talked to Jeckel, telling him to pay attention on the heeling exercise and not to look at the audience and not to sniff the ground or stop to squirt, and to go all the way down on his drop on recall, and if he moved one hair while she was out of sight on the long sits and downs, she was going to kill him with her bare hands and rip off his toenails one by one and pull his tail from the inside out. Jeckel and I both laughed at her.

She was trying to make jokes, but she was pretty nervous, I could tell.

When we got into the line of cars going through the fairground gate, I handed her father my two dollars to get in. He said, "That's okay, Dory. I've got it."

"I can pay my own way," I said, hard.

Robin said, "This is your reward for helping me with the training all summer, Dory."

That made it okay then. I sat back and got happy, and shot a look over at Meredith. She was ignoring me so I ignored her right back.

Each car had to stop as it went through the gate while a man in an apron bent over and looked in and said how much it was to get in. Robin waved her wristband at him, and her dad paid for the rest of us. The man gave us a program out of his apron pocket and said, "Good luck in your dog show, Robin. I'll be rooting for you again this year if I get off duty in time to come watch."

That made me feel like I was with a famous person. I smiled at her and she smiled back but it was stiff. She was getting more scared.

It seemed funny to think of her being scared of anything. She had so much on her side, being smart and little and cute and having a good family and a regular house and plenty of money—what did she have to be afraid of?

"Don't be scared," I whispered to her.

"I'm afraid we're going to lose tonight," she said.

"But you can't lose anything," I explained. "You might not win the trophy again this year, but you can't lose anything. See, you already got three trophies from other years and you can't lose them. So you can't *lose* anything. You can just win another one or not win another one. See?"

She stared at me for a long time, but didn't say anything, so I figured I must have said something stupid again.

Men with toy canes were waving at us, where to go to park. Robin's dad yelled to one of them, "Dog show," and the man smiled and pointed back to the corner of the fairgrounds and said, "I think there's still some parking space back there. Good luck."

The whole fairgrounds was filled with about a million cars. I didn't see how her dad could find his way around, but he did. We went around the midway where the Ferris wheel was turning and flashing its lights way over our heads, and we went past the long long barns with their doors open and lights on inside, where 4-H kids and their families were leading cows in fancy leather halters. Back at the end of the fairgrounds were some smaller buildings for sheep and rabbits and poultry, and that's where we parked and got out.

There was the building where the dog show would be. It was just a big roof, no walls. There were bleachers along both long sides, but outside the roof. The whole inside of the building would be for the dogs. It was where the training classes were held, so I knew about it from those three times I took Bingo.

Tonight it looked different. All the lights were on under the roof, and Mrs. Holland, the teacher, was standing in one corner beside a table. Robin went over to Mrs. Holland to check in, and Meredith and the parents wandered off across the way to look at the booths that were selling stuff. I decided to stay and watch Robin get ready.

Lots of the kids were already there, leading their dogs around the ring, letting them sniff the ground to get used to it or else making them heel or sit or stand or lie down, probably whatever their dogs needed to practice the worst. Robin and Jeckel went out with the rest of them and started to practice.

The dog show was supposed to start at six-thirty. When it got closer to that time, people started climbing up into the bleachers around me, getting ready. Robin's mom and dad and Meredith came back and sat down in front of me, kind of with me and kind of not. That was okay. They were mostly thinking about Robin, smiling to her and making motions that meant "Go get 'em, kid, we're with you."

I started making a play in my mind about me being their daughter instead of mom's, and having a smart dog instead of a coonhound. They would come to the fair to cheer me on, and hug me after I did good.

Plays like that make me happy on the top layer but sad on the underneath layer because they are impossible, so I don't do them very often. The play about me and Robin having an apartment together is possible, so it doesn't make me sad as much.

It finally got to be six-thirty. Mrs. Holland turned on a little switch on the metal box on her table, and that made the loudspeaker work. She picked up a microphone with a long cord and said her speech.

"Good evening, one and all. Welcome to our eighth annual Winneshiek County 4-H Dog Show. I'm Marcia Holland, the instructor, and I'd like to introduce our judge for the evening, Mrs. Dennis Fisher of Mariden Kennels. Before we start, I'll just explain a little bit about how these young trainers have worked with their dogs through the summer, and what the judge will be looking for in her scoring."

She went on, but I quit listening. Meredith's head was right down there by my knee. Should I try to tell her now. I thought. No, Robin's mom and dad might hear. And besides, Meredith was looking around at the people, probably looking for boys to flirt with. She was supposed to be thinking about Robin.

Then the first class started, and I got all interested in that. The first class was eight kids, most of them younger than me and Robin. They were the ones that had only been in it one year. When Mrs. Holland said a name, the kid would come out and start heeling, following the judge's commands to forward, halt, left turn, about-turn, speed up, slow down. The dogs were supposed to go right beside the kid's left leg, but most of them pulled against their leashes and sniffed the ground, or forgot to sit when the leg stopped walking.

Then the two posts came out and stood facing each other, eight feet apart. The posts were two of the kids' dads, I thought. They stood there grinning at each other, but one of them kept dropping his hands down at his sides. I knew better than that. When you're a post, you're supposed to keep your arms folded across your chest so the dog won't be tempted to stop and sniff your hand. I know that. I would have been a better post than that man.

After they did their figure eights around the post men, the kids made their dogs stand up and not move while the judge came up and touched the dogs. Lots of them flunked that part. Then they got away from their dogs and told them to come, and the dogs were supposed to come straight to them and sit right in front of their feet. Most of the dogs came when they were supposed to, but one little dog came so fast he ran right between his owner's feet and straight out of the ring. Everybody laughed, including the little girl, but she was trying not to cry, too. I felt so sorry for her.

After all of the kids in that class had their turns, they all came back in the ring and lined up in a row to make their dogs sit still for one minute, and then lay still for three minutes. Lots of them flunked that part.

Then the judge added up their scores, and the one that got the best score got a purple ribbon and a trophy, and all the rest got a red ribbon or a blue ribbon, depending on if they did pretty good or pretty bad.

Then they did the next class. It was the same, but for kids in their second year of training, and they had to do everything without leashes on their dogs.

Then, finally, when I didn't think I could wait any longer, it was Robin's class, for kids with three or more years. Robin was the first one to be called. I looked

down at Meredith to make sure she was paying attention, and she wasn't! She was leaning over behind
Robin's mom, and whispering to some stupid boy. I got
so mad at her right then, I didn't mind a bit what I
was about to do to her.

5 The judge said, "Are you ready?"

Robin stood straight as a string with Jeckel sitting nice and square beside her left foot, twisting his neck to look up at her. She nodded yes. I could tell she was nervous, but not as bad as most of the other kids had been.

"Forward."

She marched out, and Jeckel stayed right with her through all the halts and turns and about-turns. Then Robin took off the leash and they heeled again. This time he slowed down a couple of times but not too bad, and he kept right up with her around the figure-eight posts, speeding up on the outside corners and slowing down on the inside corners just perfect.

The judge said, "Exercise finished," just like I said it at home, practicing, and Robin bent down and scrubbed Jeckel's ears with her hands and he wagged all over.

The judge said, "Stand your dog, and leave him when you're ready."

Robin got him standing up, and fiddled around with his back legs awhile till he looked like he was standing so square he'd never want to move. Then she stood up and faced forward, gave him the signal with her hand that meant not to move, and marched three steps forward. She turned to stare Jeckel in the eye to hold him from moving while the judge went up to him and brushed her hand over his head, shoulders, and butt. He didn't move a hair.

"Return to your dog," the judge said, and Robin marched back around Jeckel's tail end and stood even with his shoulders just like she was supposed to.

"Exercise finished."

He got more hugs and ear scrubs. I looked down toward Meredith to say didn't they do good, and would you believe it, she wasn't even paying any attention to Robin. She was still talking to that stupid boy. I was so mad.

I nudged her with the toe of my shoe and said, kind of crabby, "Pay attention. Here comes the hard part."

Meredith looked at me like where did I come from, outer space, and the boy gave me a funny look and started talking to somebody else. I thought, Good.

Robin and Jeckel were standing clear down at the far end of the ring, and I could see how stiff her shoulders were. The judge gave the signal, and Robin put her hand in front of Jeckel's nose to tell him to stay, and she marched straight down the middle of the ring clear to my end. She turned and stood facing Jeckel but watching the judge.

"Call your dog."

"Jeckel, come."

He started trotting toward her. When he was halfway the judge raised her hand, and quick as a shot Robin raised her arm to signal Jeckel to lie down. He slowed up, took another step or two, but then he dropped down on his belly and pushed his head clear down to the ground to help hold himself from coming toward her like he wanted to so bad.

The judge nodded, and Robin yelled, "Jeck, come!"

He came tearing, bumped into her legs with his nose, but then sat down square in front of her like he was supposed to.

"Finish," the judge said, and Robin made a slicing motion with her hand, sideways. Jeckel hopped up and swung his butt around so he was sitting by her side again.

"Exercise finished."

Everybody started breathing again and lots of us clapped. I was so proud of her, teaching him like that and having the nerve to get out in front of everybody and do it. I knew right then, even if Bingo had been

58

able to learn all that stuff, I never would have had the nerve to be in the dog show and have everybody watch me and think, there goes that fat dummy out there making a fool of herself.

There were five other kids in Robin's class. Only two of them got the drop on recall part right. The other ones, their dogs either didn't lie down or else they didn't come at all when they were called. And none of them heeled as well as Jeckel except for one little shelty that heeled just perfect. It did the drop on recall, too, so I knew it might beat Jeckel.

After they all had their turns, they came back in and lined up along the edge of the ring, on the far side from where I was sitting. When the judge told them, they all gave their dogs the sit-stay command and walked across the ring toward my side, then turned and marched out, single file, clear out of the ring and out of sight behind the building with the rabbit cages in it. I held my breath. It was easy enough for Jeckel to do this at home, with nobody else around and Robin right there behind the lilac bush. But here, wow. There were five other strange dogs all in a row, not two feet apart from each other and nothing keeping them from ripping each other's hearts out except that command, sit-stay.

It was only supposed to last three minutes, but I swear to God it had to be ten before the judge gave the signal with her arm and they all filed back in again. All the dogs were still right where they were supposed to be. I was hoping the shelty would have moved, but it didn't.

ʼ Then they had to do the same thing again, but lying down this time, and for five minutes instead of three. Jeckel lay there looking like he was about to pop up any second. One big yellow dog stretched out on his side and went to sleep. A red one, I think an Irish setter, didn't get up but he started crawling on his elbows toward the dog next to him, which was the shelty. She watched him come for about half a minute, getting closer by inches, and then she took off across the ring. The judge's helper caught her by the collar and held her and petted her. Everybody sighed, "Ohhhh . . ." because she would have won, up till that mistake. I took about half a second to feel sorry for the girl that belonged to the shelty, but then I went back to saying yay inside, for Robin.

When the scores were added up the judge took the microphone and said, "In this class, two hundred is a perfect score. Starting from the bottom of the placements, in fourth place, Eric Hames and Rounder." Applause from his relatives as Eric came forward for his ribbon.

"Third place, Angela Wilke and Buffy, score of one hundred fifty-two." More applause. "Second place, Kim Norstrand and Misty, one sixty-eight." Lots of applause for the girl with the shelty. She looked happy.

But Robin was beaming the biggest smile you ever saw in your life. "First place, with the highest score of the evening, Robin Gorsuch and Jeckel, one hundred ninety-four."

I wanted to run right down there, but I thought I'd better not. Robin was hugging her trophy and her dog and Mrs. Holland and her mom and dad, and the man from the newspaper was trying to get her to stand still for her picture.

People started getting up and leaving the bleachers, so Meredith and I were just about alone up there. Now was my chance. My throat got dry and tight, and I couldn't remember how I had decided to lead up to it. But I knew I better say it pretty quick or I'd lose my chance.

I leaned over and said in her ear, "I bet you're glad she's your friend, aren't you?"

She kind of flinched away from me like I was a face fly, and muttered, "Sure."

"But Robin doesn't really like you."

That got her attention. She twisted around and gave me the dirtiest look I ever saw. She didn't say anything though, so I went on with my speech.

"She told me. She said she used to like you more than anybody, but lately you were getting too stuck-up and too boy crazy. And I bet she saw you sitting up here talking to that boy when you were supposed to be watching her. She knows a best friend wouldn't do that."

"You're off your rocker, Dory." She said it snotty.

I just shook my head and looked her right in the

eye. I never knew I could tell a lie that good. It halfway scared me because I never wanted to be a liar and it wasn't very nice to find out I could do it so good.

Meredith sat there staring straight ahead and ignoring me, but it looked like what I said was sinking in, because after a minute or two she said, "Robin never said that."

"She did too."

"When, then?" Snotty again.

"Yesterday when I was over there helping her train Jeckel. Just before you got there. She said you might be getting a car for your birthday and if you did you'd want her to ride to school with you next year but she didn't really want to because all you ever talked about was yourself and your boyfriends. And she wished she could ride the bus with me like we used to."

I sat back. There, I thought, that's half of it done.

After Robin got done being famous, they all started out toward the midway. I didn't know if they wanted me to go with them or not, but I was afraid of getting lost without them so I followed along behind. Robin led Jeckel and hugged her trophy and never stopped smiling.

The trophy was wood and gold, about a foot tall, with a dog on the top of it. When she showed it to me I said, wasn't it funny they put a coonhound on the trophy when coonhounds were too full of other instincts to learn obedience lessons? She looked from me to the trophy like she hadn't noticed what kind of dog it was, and then started laughing.

Robin's mom kept saying what a dinky little midway it was that year, but it was the first one I ever saw, and I thought it was wonderful. You walked around in a big circle and had to step over big fat electric cables all over the ground. On the inside of the circle were the rides, and on the outside were little tents with their sides open and games inside. I wanted to play every one we passed, but I was afraid if I stopped I'd lose the rest of them and I might not be able to find the car alone. But there were rifle shooting games and throwing darts at balloons and a lot of video games. I never saw one in person before, and I really wanted to stop and play some.

A couple of tents sold jewelry, real cheap. You could get a diamond ring for twelve dollars, and silver rings with big bluish-green stones for three and a half. And the food! You wouldn't believe it. Hot dogs a foot long, and corn dogs and brats and chili pups and cotton candy. Now that was something. I stood and watched a guy make that. He was in a white and glass wagon with yellow light bulbs around the top, and a big glass cage that had pink fluff around the edges inside it. When somebody ordered a cotton candy, the man opened the cage door and took a long paper cone and just started twirling the cone around the inside of the cage and first thing you know, there was a wad of pink fluff as big as your head stuck on that paper cone.

The man looked at me and said, "Better have some cotton candy, honey. It ain't a county fair without cotton candy."

"How much?"

"Fifty cents."

"Yes, please."

When he handed me down my fluff cone I just started at it. It was too big to get my mouth around and darn near too pretty to eat. I stuck my tongue onto it, and the fluff melted against my tongue and got like wet lumps of sugar. It was the best taste I ever tasted.

I had to walk fast to catch up with the rest of them. It was hard enough eating that thing, but eating and walking and not tripping over cables, that was almost too much. I ended up pulling long hunks of fluff off the cone just by wrapping my tongue around a little bit of it. First thing I knew, I had pink sticky chunks on my nose and chin and cheeks. I started to be embarrassed, but then Robin's dad winked at me and said, "Only way to enjoy cotton candy is dive in up to your eyebrows," and that made me feel better.

I didn't go on any of the rides. They looked too scary except for the ones that were too babyish. Robin and her dad went on the Ferris wheel, but it almost made me sick just watching them from down on the safe ground. That flimsy basket they sat in didn't have any front to it at all, just a skinny little bar across their laps, and every time the wheel stopped, their basket rocked back and forth. I couldn't hardly stand to watch them. Instead I held Jeckel's leash and told him how wonderful he was, and finished off my cotton candy down to licking the paper cone.

After we got once around the midway circle, Robin's mom said she wanted to go through the crafts building and look at the quilts and all that stuff. Her dad said he wanted to go through the barns, and Robin and Meredith both said that stuff was boring boring boring; they wanted to go watch the rock band in the grandstand for a while.

What I wanted to do was stay with Robin, but I thought maybe if I left them alone they might get in a fight over what I told Meredith, and if they did, then I wouldn't have to do the worst part, telling Robin that Meredith didn't like her. So I said I'd take Jeckel and the trophy and go with Robin's dad, since I figured he'd hate me tagging along the least of any of them.

The barns were real long, with cement floors and bright lights and everything painted white. There were pens on both sides of the aisles, and lots of kids in 4-H shirts sitting around on big fancy trunks that had the names of their farms on them. One was Rolling Acres. That made me have a picture of a whole big pasture peeling away from the earth and rolling down a giant hill. And there were pretty names like Green Valley Farms and Forest Ridge.

I stopped and asked one boy what was in the trunk he was sitting on, and he said it was brushes and hair spray and stuff like that, for his cows. Can you imagine a cow with hair spray on? I thought about a cow with curls all over her head and pink hair ribbons, and I got to giggling, but I didn't let the boy see. I didn't want to hurt his feelings.

There was a barn for dairy cattle and one for beef cattle, and barns for horses, hogs, sheep, goats, white rabbits with brown ears, and roosters every color of the rainbow, all shimmery greens and golds. I never saw a thing in the world as beautiful as those roosters.

The cows were pretty, too. Their heads were so wide and flat they were almost like table tops, and their eyes were so huge and soft. I stopped to pet one of them on her nose, and she stuck her long thick pointy tongue out and wrapped it around my wrist for a taste of my skin. It was the driest, scratchiest tongue you can imagine.

Some of the sheep were getting beauty treatments. I stopped and watched one man whittling away on his sheep with electric clippers, just like an artist making a statue. He'd shave off a little wisp of wool and then stand back and squint to see if his line was straight down the sheep's hind leg. The sheep looked bored out of its mind.

I followed Robin's dad through where they had displays of farm machinery and windmills that made electricity and the newest kinds of hog shelters and stock trailers. I don't know why he was so interested in that stuff. He worked for an insurance company.

We stopped and got barbecue sandwiches and soda

pop and kept walking while we ate, which wasn't easy, with holding Jeckel's leash and keeping him from getting tangled in people's legs. Robin's dad carried the trophy, which helped.

When I asked him how come he was so interested in all the farm stuff, he said, "I grew up on a farm, Dory, down south of Ossian." The way he said it made me think he was sad.

"Do you miss it?"

He nodded a little bit and said, like he was talking to himself, "You're always the happiest when you're young. You spend your whole life looking back on it."

I couldn't believe that. The more I thought about it the sadder it made me feel. If this was the best my life was going to be, it didn't seem like it was going to be worth the effort. And if somebody like Robin's dad couldn't make the kind of life he wanted for himself, what chance did I have?

Robin's mom was waiting for us back at the car. Then we waited a long time for Robin and Meredith before they finally came walking toward the car through the rows of other cars.

I held my breath and stared to see if they had their fight yet, but it sure didn't look like it to me. They were laughing and kind of weaving and bouncing off each other's shoulders and hips, pretending like they were drunk.

If they had a mother like mine, they wouldn't think it was so cute.

Watching them with their arms around each other's shoulders, I got such a big hurt inside me I couldn't hardly stand it. It didn't seem like I was ever ever *ever* going to get a friend I could act silly with.

They dropped Meredith off at her house, but they didn't drive up Nordness to drop me off at mine. They just expected me to walk home from their house like always.

Not that I cared about the walking. It just seemed like, there I was all cleaned up and dressed up and gone out with them for the evening, and they should have at least made the politeness of driving me home like they did Meredith.

See, that's what I mean about people thinking if you're a little bit slow upstairs, and a little bit too chubby, you don't have any feelings. I get so mad sometimes.

6 Next morning I was sitting on the bridge hanging my feet over when Robin's mom and dad drove across on their way to church. They waved and smiled at me, and I waved and smiled back.

It makes your butt feel so funny when a car goes over the bridge, because the boards bounce up and down and the whole bridge shivers. It's fun, but not very many cars ever go over the Nordness bridge so it doesn't do any good to sit there in the hope that one will go by.

I was so glad when her folks went to church without Robin. It gave me my chance. I felt kind of better and kind of worse about doing this to Robin than when I did it to Meredith, because for one thing I wasn't scared of Robin like I was of Meredith, but on the other hand I hated to make her feel bad. And I knew it was going to make her feel bad for a little while, till she switched over from Meredith to me.

But then, I was going to make it all up to her, because I would be such a better friend than Meredith ever was. I would never talk to a boy while Robin was doing her dog show.

After the car went past I sat there quite awhile, getting up my nerve. But then I got worried that church would let out and they'd be coming home before I got it done, so I got up and brushed off my butt and went across the road and up to Robin's back door. Jeckel was laying on the deck chewing a big fatty steak bone. I reckoned that was his trophy. He growled at me till I told him I didn't want his bone, then he went back to chewing and muttering under his breath about it. I knocked and Robin came to the door.

She was wearing a nightshirt kind of thing that looked like a football uniform, with stripes on the sleeves and numbers on the chest. She had her bare feet on, and her hair was all wrinkled up from sleeping. She looked contented.

For a quick flash I thought how wonderful it would be not to be scared out of your mind because the first day of school was two days away. I would have given anything for that, right then. Just to get away from the scaredness once.

"Hi, Dory, you're up and around early this morning."

She was in such a good mood she even opened the door and stood back for me to come in. Then she turned away and slouched back to the kitchen like she expected me to follow her, so of course I did.

She was eating breakfast. Cantaloupe and toast with honey on it. I stared at the cantaloupe and wondered if it tasted anything like as pretty as it looked. If anybody at my house ate any breakfast, it was only cereal or crackers or a hunk of bread. I think one reason I wanted to be a waitress so bad was just that all those different kinds of food were so pretty. Not to mention delicious, but pretty would have been enough.

Robin pointed me to a chair and I sat down, still looking at that quarter-moon of cantaloupe. The colors of it were perfect together, that rich orange and the green band inside the ring, and then the soft grayish tan of the rind. If a person wanted to decorate a room or make an outfit of clothes, all they'd have to do is look at what colors were together in natural things, and that's all they'd have to know. It's just people that make clashes, not nature.

Robin quit scooping melon into her mouth and said, "Did you want something special, Dory?"

I did, but I couldn't think of what words to say first, and while I was trying to sort them out, she butted in.

"That was fun last night, wasn't it? I thought sure that shelty had us beat; her heeling was so much better than Jeck's and she never breaks on the stay commands. Kim was so disappointed. I really felt sorry for her. I wasn't as nervous this year as usual, you know why? I kept thinking about what you said, you know, about how I couldn't lose anything, I could only win another trophy or else not, but I couldn't *lose* anything. That really helped."

That made me feel so good. She was talking to me like a friend already. She probably wasn't thinking of it being me, sitting there. She probably was just spilling over her happiness from last night and I just happened to be there, but still it felt good. I smiled and smiled at her.

Then she finished eating and started looking like she wished I'd leave so she could do whatever else she wanted to do in her morning. I knew I was going to have to get my words out. Now or never.

"You know what Meredith told me last night?" I said. My breath was coming out funny.

"No, what?" Robin started picking up her dishes and rinsing them off in the sink. Then she put them in the dishwasher.

But I made my mind get back where it was supposed to be.

"She told me she thinks you are babyish. And not pretty enough to be her friend." I looked down to my lap.

"What?"

When I looked up Robin was leaning against the sink with her hands on the counter edge and her elbows sticking out like butterfly wings. Her mouth was hanging open and showing all that metal of the braces.

When I didn't say anything, she said, "I don't believe that, Dory."

I nodded yes and said, "That's what she said. She said it was babyish to do all that dog training stuff in 4-H instead of chasing boys like her. And," my voice hard, "she said when she went to school in her new car, she didn't want a metal-mouth riding with her, scaring off the boys."

"What!" This time Robin almost yelled, and I could see that some of her mad was switching from me to Meredith. I jumped up and down inside myself, cheering that it was going to work.

"And something else," I said, looking right at her because this part was the truth, "last night when you were doing your part of the dog show, she was talking to some boy and she didn't even pay attention to you."

She didn't say anything. I think she knew it was true. She'd been glancing over at us just before she started her heeling, so she probably saw.

Gently I said, "*I* was watching you."

I wanted her to know she still had a friend even if it wasn't Meredith. That's the main thing, just to have one.

She got real quiet, thinking about everything I said, and pretty soon her face started getting kind of red and sweaty-looking, and her eyes got red edges around them. It made me want to hug her and rock her like I did Bobby when he cried, but I was afraid she might not want to be hugged by Dory Kjellings. So I just sat there helping her feel sad.

After a minute she turned around with her back to me and said, "You better go home now, Dory," just like she used to when we were little girls playing in the yard and it was time for her to go in for supper.

So I went out of her house, but I didn't go home. I went up the Nordness road toward my house, in case she was watching, but when I got past my house to where the road ends, I went around behind the old dead store buildings and back toward the horse pasture.

It was a nice breezy morning and the horses were in a better mood than the last time I visited them because the face flies weren't pestering them, but I didn't stop for any more than just hi to each of them and an extra pet for the pony. I went straight across that end of the pasture, as far from Robin's window view as I could get without walking in the bean field.

When I got to the track bed, I climbed the embankment and went down the other side and circled back toward the train station. I wanted to get there first. There was a patch of gooseberry bushes right behind the station, so I went back behind them and sat down on the ground to wait.

I sat back against a tree and set my eyes at watching where Robin would come over the embankment, and then at where Meredith would come in sight walking down the track from her house. They might not come, I knew. Or it might be a long time. I smacked a mosquito on my ankle and he squished his blood all over my skin. But then it was my blood in the first place.

Good thing Meredith only has a school driver's permit, I thought. Otherwise she could drive anywhere she wanted to in that car, and her and Robin could probably do their private talking somewhere else than where I could listen in. Like driving along the road. It was really going to be empty around Nordness when Robin and Meredith could leave me.

I did a play in my mind about how free and wonderful it would feel to have a car. And money for gas. You could go anywhere you felt like! You could just open up that door and sit down on that comfortable seat and work your hands and feet a little bit, and without hardly trying at all you could be in Decorah or Des Moines or Minneapolis or New York City!

Like a book they read to us in the special school, about Ali Baba and the forty thieves. Everybody in that book was always flying around on their magic carpets, and I used to make plays about that all the time. It seemed like if you could fly through the air like that, just by wishing it, then you would just naturally have the power to get anything you wanted, even if it was to be smart or skinny. If you had that much magic power, you could do it.

Sometimes it almost seemed like it was true, too. Here was Meredith, with her magic carpet car. They gave it to her for her birthday. Can you imagine that? Just gave it to her. She didn't have to do a darn thing to get it except have rich folks and a birthday. It was her own magic carpet. And right along with it, she was smart and skinny and beautiful. And not afraid of anything.

She didn't even have to be nice. That was what made me madder than anything, when I thought about it. It wasn't fair. She never did nice things for anybody. She never helped Mrs. Petersen take in her laundry in the mornings. She never took care of little kids for her mom, or fixed meals or anything. And yet people still made a fuss over her. She didn't even have the politeness of watching Robin in her dog show instead of talking with that boy, and yet she still got to be Robin's best friend. And she didn't *earn it*. It made me want to scream.

I earned it so hard, all the time, and I never got it.

A lot of time went by. It was way after lunchtime, I knew that. My belly growled for a while; then it gave up on me feeding it anything, and shut up. I did eat a few gooseberries off the bush in front of me, but they were mostly still green and puckery tasting, and the ones that had gone purple were too soft and sweet.

I thought about a school that had so many rich kids in it that they had to have such a thing as a school driver's permit. That thought made me sick at my stomach again. Kids that had their own cars, or even enough cars in their family so they could drive to school instead of riding the bus, well, I didn't like to admit to myself that I hated them, but in a way that's what I felt like. Because I knew they hated me first.

Well, not hated. They didn't have to hate me because they were on top. They could just ignore me like I wasn't important enough to bother with, or else they could make fun of me if they felt like it. And I couldn't do a darn thing about it. I just had to keep on being Dory Kjellings and *standing it* until I could get out of that school and into my waitress job. Then it would be okay, because they wouldn't be all the time comparing me with the other kids like in school. I wouldn't have to read fast and keep straining my head all the time trying to keep up.

But first I was going to have to face that first day in that four-story high school building with all those rooms and a thousand kids, and find my way around in it, and not fail any of my classes.

Because I could feel it inside me—if I failed at that school it was going to be the end of me. It was already wearing me out, just fighting my scaredness to get past that first day. After that it was going to be day after day of fighting scaredness, on top of all that concentration to read fast enough so I didn't just slip behinder and behinder like in elementary school. And on top of that I was going to have to clench myself up not to hear when somebody said, "Dumb Dory," or laughed if I did something clumsy or said something stupid.

And furthermore than that, those eighth grade boys and those eighth grade girls were going to be pairing up with each other. I knew it. They'd be flirting with each other behind their notebooks and in the halls by their lockers, and the ones that didn't get flirted with were going to feel awful. And of course I would be one of them.

When I added up all the bad things that were going to start day after tomorrow, it made me feel like it was the end of my life coming at me. I was going to be awful in that new school, so bad they'd send me back to the special school, and even if I ever got out of that place it would just be because I got eighteen, not because I really graduated. And then what kind of a decent restaurant would hire me? None. And it would all just get to be too heavy for me to carry, and I'd end up like my mom, just sitting in the same chair all day every day, staring out the window at the street of Nordness where no cars ever went by, and turning off her mind and waiting for her life to be over with, so she could just lie down and never get up again.

Tears started stinging up in my nose at the wanting in me. Wanting a good life for myself. It didn't really have to be bubble bath and cantaloupe. Just, *God*, just not like my mom.

I almost didn't see Robin's head popping up over

the embankment. I held real still, figuring she couldn't see through the tangles of the gooseberry bush as long as I didn't make a move. She came across the track bed and jumped down the other side, and went in to the hay room. About five minutes later here came Meredith down the track. I waited till she was inside, then I crawled out and got up beside the big open door at the end. I sat against the building, right around the corner from the big open door.

Meredith said, "What's up?"

"I just wanted to tell you," Robin said in a funny, stiff voice, "you don't have to take me to school in your car if you don't want to. I can always ride the bus."

I jumped up and down inside myself. It was working!

"What do you mean? Why wouldn't I want to? What are you talking about, Rob?"

"Oh, nothing. I just figured you wouldn't want an immature metal-mouth like me tagging along, that's all."

"What?"

"You can probably find somebody prettier, if you want boy bait, but I'll tell you one thing, if you start running around with somebody really beautiful, you're not going to look all that great by comparison. Just remember that."

"Well," Meredith snapped, "I guess Dory was right. I guess you think I'm stuck-up and boy crazy. I didn't believe her when she said that because I figured you and me were best friends and you wouldn't think something like that, or even if you did, you wouldn't tell somebody like Dory Kjellings. But I guess I was wrong."

"Wait a minute," Robin said. "Whoa a minute. Back up and run that by me again. Dory said? Dory said what? And when?"

They were quiet for a minute.

"Last night at the dog show. Dory said you said I was stuck-up and boy crazy. Isn't that what you said to her?"

There was another quiet time. I guess Robin was sorting it out in her mind. My stomach fell about six feet while I waited.

"No," Robin said finally, kind of soft and thoughtful. "Mare, I never said anything like that. Not to Dory or anybody else. I never thought anything like that. Honest to God. You know me better than that."

"Then why did Dory say that?"

"Mare, did you tell Dory that you thought I was babyish because I was still in 4-H?"

"No. God, no."

"You never said you didn't want me riding to school with you because I was so ugly I'd scare away the boys?"

Both their voices were getting higher and higher now, like the scare was over.

"No, Rob. My God, is that what . . . is that why you called me? Did that creep tell you I said that?"

I shrunk way back in myself.

They were half laughing with the relief of it now, but half mad, too.

"Why did she say those things?"

"Why would she . . . ?"

There was a thinking quiet between them again, and then Robin said, "Poor Dory."

"What do you mean, poor Dory. That creep just tried to sabotage our friendship, Rob. And darn near did it, too. If we hadn't known each other so well and trusted each other, we would have just believed her and split up, and she would have won. But I can't figure out why. I mean, what good would it do her? Do you think she was just being bitchy because she's jealous? I know she doesn't have any friends herself. But then, what does she expect?"

I tried real hard not to cry right then.

Robin said, kind of cool, "Dory is a person, Mare. Why shouldn't she at least expect to have a friend? God knows she doesn't have much else in her life. I really feel sorry for her sometimes, she seems so lonesome. But, heck, I can't carry her on my shoulders. I mean, she doesn't fit into my life anywhere and I can't . . . I just can't help her. You know? I wish she had friends of her own, but I can't do anything about it. And she does get on my nerves sometimes, I have to admit."

"She drives me up a tree," Meredith said in a flat voice.

They thought together for a while more. Then

Robin said, "I bet it was because she wanted to ride to school with us and we wouldn't let her. Do you suppose?"

"Who knows? I think she's just off her rocker."

"No"—Robin sounded careful—"she's not crazy. I wonder if maybe she's just scared about starting in a new school and she was trying to break us up so I'd ride the bus with her. You know how hard she tried to get us to take her with us in your car."

"Nah. That doesn't make sense. What's to be that scared of? School is school. Heck, I can hardly wait. Summers drive me nuts, stuck out here in the boonies."

"Yeah, but you're not Dory. Look at it from her point of view."

"Impossible. I can't think that stupidly."

"Maybe I should ride the bus with her, just that first day."

I got all stiff with hope.

"I mean, it wouldn't kill me, after all."

"Rob, you can't."

"Why not?"

"It'd be like giving in to her. You can't let her manipulate you like that, buddy. If you do, you're never going to get her off your neck. And besides, she did something really rotten to us. You want to reward her for that?"

They were quiet a whole long time, balancing my life in the air between them. I could almost see it.

Then Robin sighed a very long sigh. "I guess you're right."

They went home after that, but I sat in the weeds behind the train station till almost dark. It took too much strength to get up and keep trying.

7 Sometimes I wished I was really really dumb, so dumb my mind wouldn't work at all. That Sunday night my mind just wore me out. All I could think of was day after tomorrow. Getting on that bus at eight in the morning, strange driver, strange kids, all looking at me and thinking, there's that fat dumb girl. Big huge school building with four floors and all those rooms and a thousand rich kids. I didn't even know where I was supposed to go first. I'd get in the door and just stand there, while everybody else knew where to go.

I wouldn't even know where the bathrooms were in that building, or anything.

And no Robin.

If Robin was with me, she'd talk and make jokes, and people would see that I was her friend so I couldn't be too bad of a person in spite of how I looked. And we'd go through that front door and right to wherever we were supposed to be, and along the way she'd show me where the rest rooms and the principal's office were, so I'd have safety places in my mind.

After supper I tried to get my mind off it by watching the movie on television. It was about the big bomb going off and how the whole world would just frizzle up and die. In the commercials I said to Eldean, "Do you think it's going to happen in real life?"

"Nah," he said. "Even the Russians ain't that stupid."

I thought it might happen, though. But still, here it was Sunday night. Chances of a nuclear bomb coming before Tuesday morning didn't seem very good. Better not count on that as a way out.

Lying in bed that night between my sisters, I tried and tried to think of a way out of the mess. I was getting a headache from thinking about it, but yet I knew if I was going to figure a way out of the situation it was going to have to be pretty soon.

It was a quiet night. There wasn't any moon to speak of, so Eldean's dogs were asleep instead of baying and fussing like they did on bright nights, and Jenny wasn't wheezing in my ear like she did sometimes. So it was quiet enough to hear the mice singing.

Maybe you didn't know mice can sing. Just about everybody I tell that to says, "Dummy, mice can't sing." But they can too. On nights when there aren't other noises, I can hear them in the walls, clear as anything, singing away like crazy. The bedroom wall, where the head of the bed is up against, is right behind the kitchen cupboards, and the mice have a pathway through that wall. You can hear their little toenails scratching on the plaster, and then they sing at one another. It's real high, and maybe not everybody's ears can hear up that high, I don't know. But it sounds just exactly like a canary. Mrs. Osborne used to have a canary named Belafonte, and in the summer when the windows were open you could hear him singing his little guts out. He caught cold from a draft and died.

The mice sound just as beautiful, though, and what I like more about the mice than about Belafonte is that I'm the only one that can hear them. The little kids can't and Eldean can't, but I can. So sometimes I feel like they sing for me because nobody else is nice to me. To make it more fair, you know?

And then other times I think, everybody hates mice because they get into food and chew holes in the wallboard. But if everybody could hear how pretty they sing, they'd like them better. And it's the people's fault for not appreciating the mice, it's not the mice's fault. So maybe there is something good about me after all, and it's just that everybody else doesn't recognize it. But maybe someday I'll find a person who will see how good I am, just like I can appreciate the mice singing.

I lay there in bed thinking about how much I hated not having a person. Maybe it wouldn't even have to be a friend, even though that was what I wanted most in the world. Just a person. Eldean had some friends, and he had his parole officer. Even my mom, she had her ADC caseworker who came out once a month and checked on if the little kids were getting enough to eat. And when I was going to the special school I had Mrs. Provnic; she was my home intervention worker. She came out to the house every couple of months or so and tried to talk to my mom about evaluations and progress reports, which was like talking to a turned-off television set, but at least she came so I knew somebody was interested in me even if I was just one of seventy kids in her caseload.

But now, with me being mainstreamed into regular school, I didn't even have that kind of person for my own anymore.

I lay there and lay there and thought circles of thoughts, and after a while I came to the middle of the circles and then I knew why I was so scared of going to school alone.

Partly it was the strange kids and huge building and not knowing my way around, and all of that. And being scared of getting laughed at. And remembering the complete awfulness of that day when I started first grade and wet my pants.

But way down at the bottom of the circles of fears there was one big one that I never even looked at face to face before.

It was that I was so close to giving up.

I could feel how easy easy *easy* it would be to stay home Tuesday. And the next day and the next day.

There wasn't a person in the world who would care much, one way or the other, if I just quit school right here and now. It would be so easy just not to *try* anymore, just to let my mind slip down to nothing, like Mom's. Just spend the rest of my life sitting in a chair by the window watching the horses in the pasture and not trying to do anything, ever.

Thinking about that, it was like a light coming on in my head, and all of a sudden I started not hating my mom as much as before. I used to hate her really hard, for not trying to give us kids a better life, not even doing the laundry or cleaning up the house ever, nothing but sitting there with her bottle in her hand and her mind and face turned off.

But now I was beginning to feel how strong that pull was, to be like that. I felt so damn tired of trying and failing and trying and failing, and reading everything three times before I understood it and always getting bad grades no matter how hard I tried. It seemed like that restaurant job and that little apartment, like Alice had on television, were just fading off into a dream world like all the plays I did in my head, and I wasn't ever going to get hold of them.

I don't know whether this makes sense to you, but lying there in that bed that night, I felt like I was fighting for my life. If I didn't somehow get into that school, get past that first day and get started enough so I knew I was going to be able to make it, then the weak part of me was going to win out over the part that wanted a good life for Dory Kjellings, and I was never in the world going to have enough strength to try again.

And without Robin to help me, I just plain couldn't make it. Maybe that doesn't make sense to you, and maybe it wasn't even true, but that's why I decided to do what I did.

I couldn't break up the friendship. Okay. All I really needed was Robin to help me through that first day at school. That meant getting her on that bus with me.

That meant keeping Meredith and her car away from Robin's house till after the bus came, at eight o'clock Tuesday morning. One thing I heard her and Robin talking about that afternoon in the train station was deciding to leave early Tuesday morning so they could drive around awhile and look over the crop of boys getting off the different buses.

Meredith said she'd be at Robin's house at seven-thirty. The bus would be at Robin's corner at eight.

If I could some way stop Meredith before she left home, or on the way, and then cut back by the railroad track bed, I could be at Robin's corner by eight. And if Meredith hadn't showed up yet in her car, Robin would have to ride the bus with me.

So that was it. That's what I would have to do.

How, though? I thought about doing like they do on television, ripping out wires or whatever inside the car so it wouldn't start. I wouldn't know how to do that, but maybe if I asked Eldean he'd show me.

But then I thought about that car, sitting out in plain sight between Meredith's house and the barns, right under the yard light so I couldn't sneak in in the middle of the night. Their dogs would raise hell, and anybody looking out the house windows would see me, plain as day. That's why farms all have those yard lights high up on those poles, to keep people from stealing expensive farm machinery and livestock and gas out of the gas barrels.

And by early morning her dad would be out starting the chores, so there'd be no chance then.

But if I waited till she started driving around the mile toward Robin's house . . . the road curved right about where the railroad track bed met it, and there was a woods there, so nobody could see anything from Meredith's house. And there weren't any other houses on that road, not for a long ways, and not much traffic.

If I walked up the track bed way early, and waited till her car came around, and jumped out and made her stop, and then . . . did something, I wasn't sure what, but something to keep her there, and then ran all the way back down the track bed to Robin's corner, I'd be there in plenty of time for the bus. And Meredith would be late, and Robin would get on the bus with me.

And everything would be all right.

Finally I relaxed enough to go to sleep.

. . .

By the next morning it seemed like a crazy idea. I didn't let go of it completely, but it sounded impossible and stupid when I thought it over. I got Eldean to take me into town to the Laundromat so I could wash up a whole mountain of clothes for me and the little kids, to start school in. Jenny and Angie would be going to elementary in Ossian. Bobby and the baby were too young yet.

Usually we did laundry in Ossian, which is a littler town than Decorah. It's six miles south of Nordness. But that morning Eldean needed to pick up dog food, which he got at the Farm Fleet because that was the cheapest, so we went to Decorah instead of Ossian.

He left me and the three laundry baskets off at the Koin King and went off to get his dog food. Luckily he'd just got fifty dollars from a guy that bought a pup from him last year and just finished paying for it, so I had the money for the washing machines and the dryer both. Most often we just washed there and hauled the wet stuff home and hung it on the line, but those baskets got so heavy, you wouldn't believe how much heavier wet wash is than dry. It was a luxury to throw the stuff in those big old dryers and watch it somersaulting around in there.

Eldean got back before I was finished, and he brought us each a cheeseburger in a little square plastic box, with one teeny bag of fries between us. We got Cokes out of the machine there at the laundry and had a picnic on the plastic chairs in the corner while some-

91

body's little boy climbed all over our legs and tried to get our food. It would have been a wonderful day except for all the scares in my stomach about tomorrow.

When we got the laundry all loaded in the back of the pickup on top of the bags of Kennel Crunch, I said, "Could we go around past the high school building once?"

"What you want to do that for?" Eldean said, but he drove by anyhow.

The front doors were open and there were cars parked in the parking lot at the side of the building. "Teachers' meetings today," I said.

Then an idea hit me. I grabbed his arm and said, "Dean, take me inside."

"Huh?"

"Take me in the school building once. You could show me around the place a little bit, couldn't you?"

It wouldn't be as good as going in with Robin, but if I could see inside the building and find out what room to go to first, then maybe if I chickened out with the plan for stopping Meredith, I might be okay in the morning, on my own.

Eldean looked at me like I was nuts. "I told you I'd never go inside there again. Why do you keep pestering me about it?"

"Please, Eldean?" I begged him. "I never asked you for very much."

"You ask me for stuff all the time," he snorted.

"Okay, I won't anymore if you'll just do this one thing for me. It's important."

I guess he could see how much I meant it, because he looked at me, and then his eyes got softer, and he shrugged.

"Okay, just this once, but I'm only going one step inside the front door. If you want to go any farther, you'll have to go on in alone."

He parked in the street in front of the school and we got out. I felt crummy walking toward that building in my dirty shorts and tee shirt and falling-apart sandals, and Eldean was his usual messy self and smelled a little bit like he'd been skinning coons, which he had. Halfway to the door I was ready to cut and run. But he kept going, so I did, too.

We got up the front steps and as far as the door and one step inside, into a wide wide hallway that seemed like it stretched away forever in front of us.

Then a man came out of a door to the side and saw us. He was all spiffed up in suit and tie, looking like the president or some such.

"No students allowed today." He sort of sang the words, like he'd been saying them a lot.

We stopped dead.

"No students allowed today, teachers' meetings," the man said again, tougher that time. We turned and left.

All the way home I kept telling myself the man

wasn't really unfriendly. If the rule was no students allowed in the school that day, then he had to say it. But still, it made the school seem outright unfriendly. Not just big and scary any more, but like it didn't want me inside it.

More and more I was tempted to stay home tomorrow. Give up. Was it worse to give up or to fail, I kept asking myself all evening while I sat staring at the little people jumping around on the television screen. I stayed up way after everybody else went to bed, not because I was interested in the programs, just because I couldn't seem to make myself do anything. Not go to school alone, not stop Meredith's car, not even get up off the floor and turn off the TV and go to bed.

It was some detective program that finally made my eyes go into focus. Guys kept knocking each other out, left and right. Just one hard fast punch to the jaw and the other person would slump to the floor or the ground or whatever, and be conveniently unconscious till after the commercials.

I could probably hit somebody that hard.

I could probably hit Meredith right on her chin and knock her out and then . . .

I closed my eyes and concentrated. If I jumped out in the road and made her stop her car, she would open the door or roll down the window, to yell at me to get out of the way. I could punch her on the jaw and then I could steer the car so it went in the ditch. She would be knocked out for a little while, and then she'd have to walk back to her house and get her dad to come with the tractor and tow chain and pull her car out of the ditch, and by that time Robin and I would be on the school bus.

I turned off the TV so I could think better. The idea was making me excited now.

And then when Meredith woke up maybe she wouldn't remember about me hitting her, or she'd remember it fuzzy and not be sure. People would think she just drove into the ditch because she was a new driver, and hit her head on the steering wheel.

Nobody could prove I hit her. And there wouldn't be any harm done. Cars went in the ditches all the time in winter when the roads were slick. People just went and got the nearest farmer and he'd pull the car out with his tractor and that was that.

The idea didn't seem crazy or impossible anymore. I knew, then, that I was going to do it.

8 I made myself lie in bed till almost six, even though the sky was light by five. Then I got up quiet and washed myself all over with a washrag and put on my summer dress, the same one I wore to the fair. It was pink on top, and the bottom and sleeves were pink and yellow plaid. You'd think pink and yellow wouldn't look good together, but these did. They were sort of softened into each other.

I would have felt better in jeans, especially for the running part of the plan, but I didn't know for sure if kids wore jeans to the new school so I didn't dare.

I got a piece of bread and ate it standing by the kitchen window. It made a heavy lump going down and it made me know how nervous my stomach was. I almost gave the whole thing up, right then. But I was already washed and dressed and hair-combed, and it seemed like that was enough to push me out the door. So I took my canvas shoulder bag and headed out.

The morning air is always the best of the whole day. It was like it hadn't been used yet, or breathed up, or sweated into. It smelled like dew and mist. Everything was wet, but I couldn't tell if it was from rain or just from the mist and dew. It was still misty, like it gets in these little valleys early in the morning. Up on the hill it was probably burned off already and clear blue, but the creek valley was still poured full of mist.

I went through the wires of the pasture fence and headed across the grass, jumping the creek at a narrow place and trying to look like all I was doing was saying hi to the horses if anybody was looking from any of the house windows. My tennis shoes were soaked through before I got halfway to the track bed bank. The shivering all through me made it hard to think, so I just concentrated on walking.

Up the track bed, away from Nordness and the school bus corner. Old railroad ties buried almost out of sight in the rocks under my feet. Try to walk on them and not the rocks; save my feet for the run back. Thin soles on my shoes. Even the roughness of the ties came through to my feet.

At the north edge of the pasture I had to climb over the fence because the wires were too close together to get through between. Put my toes on one strand, up close to a wood post, grabbed the post top, and swung my other leg over. Skirt was in the way. Post was loose in the ground and wobbled and almost threw me off. Pulled my skirt up and made my muscles tighter and

97

tried again. Swung over. Cut the inside of my knee on the barbs going down the other side. I was so nervous I didn't feel the hurt, but the sight of the blood rising up out of my skin and making a little river down my leg made me dizzy for a minute.

But I had to pull myself together, so I did. Walked on north. Bean fields on both sides of me now. It was like walking a long bridge across the greeny-tan ocean, all those bean plants down there with their soybean pods growing on them, making money for Meredith's father to buy her cars with.

I walked faster and faster. My mind was working clearer now, and it was focusing on Meredith. All her fault.

The track bed curved west toward the end of the bean field and went through woods. I stopped and waited while seven deer walked across the track bed in front of me. A buck, three does, one that looked like a yearling, and two this-year's fawns. They looked at me but didn't get too worked up, although they did start switching their straight-up white tails, signaling that there was a person watching them and they'd better be careful. They started bounding away then, bouncing their butts way up in the air with every jump, but they weren't going very fast, just showing me they could if they needed to.

In the woods it was so misty I could only see a few trees' worth of distance and all the rest was a white blank. The mist made it quieter, too. I couldn't hear any sounds from Meredith's house, over east of the woods.

I wished I could just turn into a deer and live in those woods the rest of my life.

But then the woods ended and there was the road up ahead, crossing the track bed. It was a narrow cream-colored gravel road with grassy ditches along it, maybe three feet deep, just enough ditch so the snow plows had someplace to push the snow into in winter.

Just enough ditch so if a car went in, it would take a tractor to pull it out again.

There was no place to sit down where I wouldn't get my dress dirty, and I was going to have to be ready when her car came around that bend, so I stood in the middle of the road.

A gravel road isn't like a blacktop or a highway. You don't have one side all to yourself to drive on, for the direction you're going. A gravel road is humped up a little bit in the middle and kind of soft and crumbly along the edges, so the only good place to drive is right down the middle, on top of the hump and away from any bad places at the edges where a rain might have made a washout. So everybody drives in the middle and you just get over to your side if you're coming toward a curve or a hill where somebody might be coming from the other way.

I stood in the middle, facing toward Meredith's house, and I waited.

In my mind I kept going over it and over it, what

to say and how to hit her and what to do with the car to get it in the ditch. The worst part to think about was the hitting. I never hurt anybody in my life. I didn't know if I could do it or not. Especially another girl. If it was a robber or somebody trying to hurt me, that would be different.

But she *was* hurting me. She talked Robin out of riding the bus with me, and she talked Robin out of letting me ride with them in her car. She didn't like me, so I didn't like her. That was the way it worked. If someone liked you, then you liked them, but you couldn't like somebody if they didn't like you. She could have liked me. She could have at least been nice to me like Robin, even if she didn't want me for a friend.

If I was her and she was me I would have been nice to me. If I had a rich father that bought me a car I would let anybody ride in it that wanted to.

It wasn't my fault I got born in the family I did, and it wasn't any credit to her that she got born in the family she did. She had all the advantages from the word go, and yet she made herself be a snotty, mean person. She didn't have to do that. I didn't have any advantages, and I would never treat other people the way she treated me.

I started breathing harder, getting all worked up about how unfair it was, and seeing inside my eyes how her face always got stiff when she looked at me, and hearing the names she called me when she talked to Robin in the train station.

100

I was so mad, standing in the middle of that road on that misty morning, that I almost forgot the reason I was there.

And then all of a sudden, before I could hardly get my thoughts back into my head, a green car was in front of me. I stood still. I forgot what I was going to do first.

Meredith's face was mad, inside the window. She waved at me to get around to the side. I stood still.

The green car stood still.

She moved to shove a gear and the car started backwards, like she was going to back up a little bit and then go around me.

All of a sudden my mind went blank but my body was moving. Fast. It was out of control. It went to the car door and pulled it open and my arms shot out and my fist started hitting. It was like for the first time in my life I was on top of the rich smart pretty people and all those hates and scares came pouring out of me and I couldn't stop them. My eyes blurred over like they were full of tears.

Meredith sagged down away from my hands, and something hit me hard on my left side, knocked me down.

I sat up and tried to get my eyes working. The green car had backed up in a curve and was sliding down off the road into the ditch. The motor was still running and the door was swinging shut. It was the door that hit me and knocked me down, I figured.

My body took over again, and when my thoughts got straightened out, I was running down the track bed through the woods, toward home. I could see that car with its nose sticking up out of the ditch, wheels still going around in slow motion.

Out of the woods, through the bean field ocean.

Her foot must have slipped off the pedal when I hit her. I knew enough about driving from watching Eldean in his truck to know that if you took your foot off one of the pedals and the truck was in gear, it would start moving, forward or backward, depending on which gear it was in. She was backing up before I hit her, so her gears were probably still in back-up.

By the time I got to the fence between the pasture and the bean field I was feeling pretty good. The scary part was done. She was in the ditch just like I planned it, and Robin would have to go in the bus with me. I got over the fence and stopped to catch my breath and look myself over. Scraped places on both of my arms, one from the car door and one from landing on the gravel. Dirt on my pink and yellow plaid skirt, and one little torn place, but the tear didn't show very much and most of the dirt would brush off when it got dry.

I fished around in my shoulder bag and found my comb, and combed my hair. Then, with about three big deep breaths under my belt, I headed out across the pasture to Robin's corner to wait for the bus.

I put out of my mind that I had just hurt somebody

and concentrated on the strong, good feeling that I was pulling myself away from ending up like my mom.

I was going to school, and Robin was going to make sure I got through the day.

9 It was ten till eight when Robin came out of her house. I know because I asked her. She looked at her watch and told me, but then she went back to looking up the road, kind of half frowning.

There was a white fence around her front yard with big white wagon wheels stuck in the ground for fanciness. I leaned on one of the wheels and Robin sat on the fence by me, looking up the road all the time. I looked down it, the other direction, where the school bus would come at eight o'clock.

"She should be here by now," Robin muttered.

"Maybe she slept late."

She shook her head. "I just called over there. Her mom said she left a long time ago. She must have had car trouble. Darn darn darn *darn*. We were going to arrive in style, first morning especially. Nuts."

I was surprised she didn't notice how scratched up and wild I was looking, but she didn't really look at me.

She was too busy looking down the road. For a second I was sorry to be the one to make her disappointed. But then I thought how much more I needed her this morning than she needed Meredith, and I forgave myself. She could ride home with Meredith after school, and they could ride to school every other morning in the car. It was just today that I needed her so bad.

Pretty soon I was counting to sixty over and over, making the minutes go by. That green car could still come over the hill from the west before the yellow school bus came down the farther-away hill from the east, and crossed the bridge and picked us up. I wasn't safe yet.

A car came from the west. I stopped breathing. But it was a brown one. It went past, and the driver waved and we waved back, me especially.

Robin got off the fence and started walking around, like her legs were too nervous to be still. "I bet she had a flat tire. I bet you anything she had a flat tire. Those back tires were both worn down to nothing on the insides. I warned her."

I just finished counting another sixty when that beautiful beautiful school bus came rolling down the far hill.

I said, "She's not here yet, Robin. You'll have to ride the bus with me."

Her forehead wrinkled up and she made a high squeaky whine sound and turned her head back and forth real fast, from the bus to where the green car

105

wasn't coming. The bus coasted over the bridge, rattling the board and cables, and rolled to a stop right in front of us. The driver looked right at us, waiting for us to hop on.

A phone started ringing, inside Robin's house. She hesitated and looked toward where the sound was coming out the kitchen window.

I grabbed her arm and pulled her toward the bus. "Come on, the driver will get mad."

"Oh . . . nuts. That's probably her calling right now."

"Come on, girls," the driver yelled out his window at us. "Got to keep on my schedule."

All across the road she muttered, "Rats and mice and fishhooks."

We got on. Having to pull her on the bus made me forget to be scared of the strange driver and strange kids. The driver had a clipboard in front of him with a list of names on it. He looked up at us and said, "I had you scratched off my list this year, Robin."

"Yeah, well, scratch me back on, today anyhow," she growled.

He looked at me. "Dory Kjellings?"

I nodded.

He smiled and pulled a lever that made the door go shut, and that was that.

Robin went into an empty seat and I sat beside her. She hunched up and looked crabby and probably she didn't want me sitting with her, but I wasn't letting her

106

get away from me. Not after everything I'd had to do to get her there. The ride to town was slow because we had to stop several more places and pick up more kids, but it wasn't scary. The other kids all had friends to sit with and talk to. They didn't pay any attention to me. That was okay. It was better than getting teased.

I tried to talk to Robin about the dog show last weekend, but she acted like that was old history and she didn't want to think about it. From her face, I guessed she was practicing what to say to Meredith about her not showing up like they planned. She looked like she was getting madder and madder.

Then we were driving through town streets, and before I could hardly get myself ready for it, we were stopped beside the school and everybody was standing up and getting out. I got right beside Robin and walked up that long wide sidewalk in step with her. My heart was pounding in my neck. The kids were like a river pouring around us, crowding in on both sides, running and laughing and pushing.

I wanted real bad to hold onto her arm, but I knew she wouldn't want that. She acted like I wasn't there, but that was okay. The main thing was just being able to walk through that door beside her and follow her to wherever we were supposed to go.

Up the steps. Everyone yelling and whooping around. It was more people than I'd ever seen in my life all in one place. We crowded in through the door, bumping shoulders with everybody.

107

The funny thing was, once I got inside I really didn't need Robin to know where to go. Everybody was going in one direction, and I just swam along with the tide. It took us into a great big room in the middle of the building, with shiny gold wood floors and rows of seats that went on forever.

We sat down. Robin was still beside me. When the whole room was filled up, a man got up on the stage at the end and talked into a microphone. You could hear him just fine. He said he was the principal, and then he gave us a nice little speech welcoming everyone. He told us if our last names began with A through D we were in the A section of our grade, E through I was in the B section, J through N was in the C section, and so on. I must have looked confused for a second because Robin whispered, "You're a C then." I was figuring it out for myself by that time so she wouldn't have had to tell me, but it was nice of her to. I smiled.

Then the principal read off a list of room numbers and what classes had their home rooms in which rooms. I listened for 8-C and memorized it when he said it. Class 8-C was in room twelve. Then people were going along the rows handing out papers all down the line. I took one and looked at it. It was a map of the school building that showed where all the rooms were, and the rest rooms and offices and library and nurse's room and everything you would ever need to know.

I stared at it.

It started coming into my head then that I wouldn't have needed Robin after all. I could have found my way around all right without her. The school people had everything all fixed so new people wouldn't get lost or scared. So that meant that I wasn't the only one that felt that way.

I wasn't the only one.

That made me feel so good. I felt strong, all of a sudden. When the meeting was over I said good-bye to Robin without hardly even looking at her, I was concentrating so hard on following my map to room twelve.

When everybody was in their right rooms, a bell rang and the teacher introduced herself and said that this would be our homeroom and we'd meet in that room for fifteen minutes every Monday morning and then go on to our regular classes. She handed out cards for each of us that told us what our class schedules were for every hour of every day, and all the teachers' names and room numbers.

So I was safe. I had my map and my schedule.

She told us that today we would just go to each of our classes and get our seat assignments and meet our teachers, but only stay about fifteen minutes in each class, and go home at one o'clock, and then start tomorrow with regular classes. She explained about how different grades, seventh through twelfth, which were all in that building, would go to lunch at ten-minute intervals so the cafeteria wouldn't be too crowded, and that sounded confusing, but she went through the explanation again and I got it the second time. At first I thought she meant we only had ten minutes to eat.

Then a bell rang again, and everybody got up and left. I took a good long look at my map and went to find my first class.

I got through everything! I got through all the morning classes and the lunch line in the cafeteria, although that was confusing. At first I didn't know I was supposed to take silverware out of the racks till I got clear to the end of the line and somebody had to tell me. And I didn't know anybody at the table where I sat, but that was okay. The main thing was I got through it.

I was in my last class of the afternoon, listening to the teacher introduce himself and explain how his name was pronounced, when a voice came out of the box up by the ceiling. It had been doing that all day, making announcements, so I didn't jump this time when it started talking.

But then I heard what it said, and after that I turned into stone.

"May I have your attention please. I have a very unhappy announcement to make at this time. May I have your attention please. I am deeply sorry to have to announce the death of one of our students. Meredith Kraus has just been pronounced dead at Decorah General Hospital, as a result of an automobile accident early this morning. Funeral arrangements will be announced later, and students wishing to attend will be excused from classes at that time. I'm sure we all extend our deepest sympathies to Meredith's family." The voice in the box sounded like it was breaking up, at the end. It clicked off.

They started talking around me but I didn't hear anything because my ears were ringing louder and louder. Then I wasn't in the room anymore. I was walking down the hall. Somebody said something to me. I could see a man's face tilting toward me, peering at me like he was looking at me through water or thick glass. His lips moved but the ringing was too loud. I couldn't hear him.

I was scared he couldn't hear me through the glass, either, so I said it as loud as I could.

"I killed her. Help me."

10 I was in a hospital for a long time after that. In the psychiatric ward. I don't remember much about that. They said I had a breakdown. Then when I got better, so I knew what was going on around me all the time, they sent me here, to Mitchelville.

It's the State Training School for Girls, like where Eldean went at Eldora, for boys. It's a great big huge place with lots of big brick buildings set around a lawn. When I first saw it it reminded me of a college campus on television. I live in one of the brick buildings. They call them cottages, but a cottage is supposed to be a cute little house and these aren't. But the people that run them, cottage parents they're called, are really nice. Even to me.

When they let me out of the hospital, I just expected everybody would hate me for the rest of my life for what I did to Meredith. That was the way it should be, I figured. I did the worst thing a person can do, and nobody should ever like me or be nice to me again.

I really expected them to put me in the electric chair.

When they brought me here to Mitchelville, they gave me a psychiatrist and a counselor besides the cottage parents, Mr. and Mrs. Card. Isn't that a funny name? Like queens and deuces and jokers. Every one of those people they gave me treated me nice. I couldn't figure out why. I didn't even want them to, really, because it wasn't right.

It was the counselor that finally got through to me. She had more time to spend with me because the cottage parents were pretty busy and the psychiatrist had to take care of about fifty screwy kids. The counselor didn't have that many.

Her name is Miss Woelke, but you say it like Welky. The first time we talked, we had a good laugh about extra wasted letters in our names, O in hers and K in mine. She is tall and skinny and wears jeans mostly, and has long straight black hair. She has the kind of face that makes you trust her.

In our first serious session, after the one where we looked each other over and talked about the letters in our names, she asked me to tell her about Meredith's accident. I started to. She never interrupted me with words, but she'd start writing things down while I was talking and that made me get off my train of thought. I tried to tell her all about why I did it, but I don't think

113

she understood. How could she, when she was writing at the same time? That's why I invented you for an imaginary listener-friend, see? You didn't once interrupt, and you didn't write things down while I told you. Thank you.

I said to Miss Woelke, "But I still don't understand how Meredith died. Nobody ever told me. Can you?"

She read some papers in a folder that had my name on it. "Cause of death," she said slowly, "was asphixiation."

"What does that mean?"

"Dory, it means she died from breathing in the car's exhaust fumes. Exhaust fumes are deadly poison, you know."

"But how could that happen? All I did was hit her. And then the car rolled backwards into the ditch. How could that make her die?"

She put her feet up on her desk and crossed her hands over her stomach. She wore moccasins, and on the soles of them you could see the shape of her foot and each toe in the worn leather. It looked funny. I wanted to think about that, not about Meredith.

"Apparently," she said, "at least from what the police report says here, after the car started rolling backward, because it was in reverse gear at the time you hit her, Meredith fell sideways and evidently knocked the gear lever into neutral position, so the car didn't stall and die as it would have done if it had still been in gear when it stopped. The door beside the

114

driver apparently fell shut, or swung shut, and the tail-pipe jammed down into the ground when the car backed down into the ditch, so the exhaust fumes were forced up into the car. Meredith apparently hit the side of her head against the window on the passenger's side of the car and that blow, not the one you gave her, stunned her long enough for the exhaust fumes to back up into the car and render her unconscious, and then kill her. It was a freak accident, Dory."

I sat and thought about it and thought about it.

She went on, in a kind voice. "Her family found her about ten minutes later, after her friend . . ."

"Robin."

"Robin, yes. After Robin called. They assumed the whole thing was an accident. They still feel that way, Dory."

I was crying when I finally looked up. It was the first time I cried since it happened. "I hit her. I was waiting for her and I made her stop the car and I hit her."

"But you didn't mean to kill her, Dory."

"I didn't mean to, but I did."

After that session we talked about the accident a lot. We still do, and I know she's trying to help me not feel guilty. But she keeps making notes when I talk, and I know she tells other people what I say, like the psychiatrist and other people at their staff meetings. She is nice to me because it's her job to be, and that's better than nothing.

She wants me to get over feeling guilty. I don't ever want to get over it. Meredith can't get over being dead, and Robin can't get over losing her friend that way, so why should I get over feeling guilty?

The only thing I can think of that makes it more fair is that Meredith gets to live with Jesus and I never will, now.

But in between thinking about that, I like living here. We get to take baths every night if we want to, and the food is lots better than at home. I go to classes in the school building, and so far I'm keeping up pretty well with my schoolwork. There aren't as many kids in the classes here, and no boys at all. That helps. The kids are all working on different levels because they start in here whenever they get sent here for getting into trouble with the law or whatever, so the teachers work with each one of us kind of separately, and I can do pretty well like that.

The best class is for sewing. You don't have to read much for that one, and some of the cloths are such pretty colors. I made myself a red blouse and white skirt with a red border around the bottom and red tulips growing out of it. It's called a border print, that kind of material. I lost a lot of weight when I had my breakdown, so now when I wear that new outfit that I made myself, I look really good, for me.

I don't hear from Robin very much, except she sent me a card at Christmas and told me she really likes school this year, and Jeckel got heartworms but he's okay now, and she doesn't think she'll show him in 4H next year. I think she outgrew it. That makes me sad.

One funny thing. Well, a nice thing. Eldean has gotten in the habit of writing me letters just about every week. He never wrote home all that time he was in Eldora, but for some reason he's been acting nicer to me than he ever did before this happened. He tells me about Double Circle's pups, and about how many coons he got that week, and how he's beginning to make some real money selling his young dogs. He got five hundred for one. Mom is the same, he says every week. I guess she will always be the same till she dies.

There is one other thing that happened here, just since I started telling you all this. I don't know if I should tell you this part. It's so good. But I know I'm not supposed to be happy any more after what I did, so I don't tell too many people how happy I am about this part of it.

I have a friend.

Her name is Lori, so we're Lori and Dory. She's in my cottage.

She's like me.

And she never had a friend before, either. Isn't that wonderful?

When I first started telling you all this, I didn't know yet if Lori wanted to be friends. But last night after supper she asked me to play Ping-Pong. I didn't know how, but she taught me, and then we talked for a long time afterwards, and she definitely wants me for her friend.

So I don't need to talk to you any more. Thank you for not interrupting me.

Good-bye.

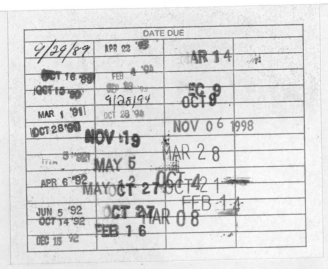